ELEGY FOR A THIEF

Also by Margaret Press

Requiem for a Postman

ELEGY FOR
A THIEF

A Detective Sergeant
Gabriel Dunn Mystery

Margaret Press

Carroll & Graf Publishers, Inc.
New York

Copyright © 1993 by Margaret Press

First Carroll & Graf edition 1993

Carroll & Graf Publishers, Inc.
260 Fifth Avenue
New York, NY 10001

Library of Congress Cataloging-in-Publication Data
Press, Margaret L.
    Elegy for a thief : a Detective Sergeant Gabriel Dunn mystery /
Margaret Press. — 1st Carroll & Graf ed.
        p.   cm.
    ISBN 0-88184-949-9 : $18.95
    1. Police—Massachusetts—Salem—Fiction.   I. Title.
PS3566.R38E44   1993
813'.54—dc20   92-47584
                                                                    CIP

Manufactured in the United States of America

Grateful acknowledgment is made to the following for permission to
reprint excerpts from previously published lyrics:
                        "OL' MAN RIVER"
        Written by Jerome Kern and Oscar Hammerstein II
    Copyright © 1927 PolyGram International Publishing, Inc.
                        Copyright renewed.
            Used by Permission. All Rights Reserved.

For
Chuckie

AUTHOR'S NOTE

I wish to acknowledge with deep appreciation the technical and moral support of the following:

Sara Press, Adrianne Lilley, Stanley Anderson, Marge Leighton, William Press, Jeffrey Howell, William Nye, Maureen Riley, Ella Roberts, Dennise Munroe, Pat Morency, Elizabeth Fleming, Cha-Cha O'Brien, Sally Hayes, John Hayes, John R. Keilty, Harold Olsen, Joan Pinkham, Michael Johnson, Norman Hawley, Linda Leighton, Alan Leighton, Richard Woodbury, Kay Dreher, Elaine Gallo, Jane Dionne, Charlotte Thompson, Paul Gangi, Jim Madsen, and Sanchez Computer Associates; and my agent, Susan Crawford.

The Salem Police Criminal Investigation Division: Det. Sgt. Conrad Prosniewski, Det. Sgt. Richard Urbanowicz, Det. Sgt. Mary Butler, Dets. James Page, William Jennings, James Gauthier, and Peter Baglioni, Capt. Paul Tucker; Salem Police Officer Nelson L. Dionne, Jr.; Michael Rosenberg, M.D.; Tom Campbell of the U.S. Postal Service, Salem, Mass.; Peter Chalapatis, Mark Bourdeau, NCCI Gardner; Robin Bavaro, Department of Corrections, Office of Public Affairs; Sonny Kinslieh, Witch's Brew Cafe; Benjamin Lewin, and David Lewin, Home Plate.

My apologies to Blueberry, and to the Perley house and its owners. The story, names and characters are fictitious, though Leslie's Retreat and North Salem's contribution to history are not.

Steal away, steal away home,
I ain't got long to stay here.

My Lord calls me,
He calls me by the thunder,
The trumpet sounds within my soul;
I ain't got long to stay here.

　　　　　—"Steal Away"
　　　　　Traditional Black American
　　　　　Spiritual, c. 1871

Chapter 1

Flight of Icarus

"Who died?" The three hundred-pound flight instructor looked up at Detective Sergeant Gabriel Dunn and slid a key across the counter. Dunn flew only to escape a case. And his inexplicable compulsion to fly was severely hampered by his tortuous relationship with his instructor. Zack wheezed and continued: "We're taking Five-Seven-Vicious. It's mostly intact."

N3857V was a bitch to start up in the cold. Saturday, January 26, was cold. Beverly Municipal Airport was strewn with windrows of old snow. "Zack. No one died," said the detective.

"Nobody dying in Salem? You'll soon be out of a job, son. How're you gonna keep paying for lessons the rest of your life?"

"I don't intend to fly with you the rest of my life, man. I'll kill myself first."

"So if you're not on a case, why the hell'd you come out?" Zack's preflight briefings were largely given to berating Dunn's infrequent-flyer program.

"Hey, lapper," lapper being a local police term of endearment, "you know how many details I endure to pay for one lousy lesson with you? And what do I get? You pump me for information, you tell me how to run my cases, you ask me to fix your tickets. You blow smoke in my face, you put the plane overgross. No wonder I can't fly."

"I never said you couldn't fly, boy. Take it easy." The fat man grunted. "It's just you gotta get up more than once a homicide, Gabe. Salem's not lethal enough. You'll never solo."

Dunn smiled and held the door open. "You're milking me, you sonofabitch."

The flight instructor persisted. "Read in the *Times* where you folks been having break-ins all week. Any suspects yet?"

"Nope," Dunn lied.

"You dust for prints?"

Dunn looked annoyed. "Never occurred to us."

"That sports card store? You find any of that poor bastard's little baseball cards?"

The pair had arrived at the single-engine Cessna 150. The detective zipped up his jacket and began loosening the tiedown ropes.

Zack leaned one large arm against the strut. "Those cards were pretty valuable, the paper said. I hope you boys get them back."

Dunn answered tightly: "OK. You're right, I am avoiding the case."

Zack formed a sad "ohhh" with his mouth. "He wasn't insured, Gabe. That's what I read."

Dunn wanted to kill him. "Well, we're stuck. The B and E's have all been clean. No traces."

"All right!" beamed the instructor. "We'll try a hammerhead stall over Plum Island. It'll all fall into place!"

Dunn winced at the metaphor. Then his beeper went off.

Moira Doheny lay in an awkward pile on the floor of her North Salem living room. One bare foot was entangled in

the leg of an overturned chair. The right side of her porce-
lain face and Victoria's Secret paisley robe were soaked
with blood. Like broken wings, the young woman's slender
twisted arms protruded from her sides, helpless in allaying
her final fall. The purple in her frail hands declared her
biologically dead.

Dunn was not happy with the scene. Moira Doheny's
death had been unattended. With unattended death come
detectives. Dunn's partner Jake Myles had been the first
detective from the Salem P.D. Criminal Investigation Division on the scene and had taken temporary charge. Myles
had preceded his sergeant by enough minutes to have had
the case nearly solved. As Dunn stood now in the middle
of the dimly lit room digesting the damage, Myles hovered
at his elbow and translated like a tour guide at the House
of Seven Gables.

"Appears to be a suicide, Gabe. No signs of forced entry. Doors were locked when the landlord found her.
You'll find the note on that desk, and a Charter Arms
revolver by her hand. Looks like a thirty-eight, a Bulldog
or something."

"You're taking pictures?" asked Dunn. "Any family
here? Where's the landlord?"

"He's waiting upstairs. There's another apartment up
there. This used to be the old Pealey place, didn't it? Anyway, we told him to stick around. No one else has showed.
No one from the State's responding, except ballistics and
the medical examiner. She should be here shortly." Myles
raised his Nikon and finished shooting the roll. "Nice-
looking girl."

Dunn crouched down beside the body. He slipped a
hand under her arm. She was still somewhat warm to the
touch, and naked beneath the robe. Without moving her
he couldn't locate an exit wound, but the bullet had entered about an inch above her right ear, streaking the bril-

liant red hair with a swatch of brunette. The right hand appeared to have powder burns. Moira's arms were still limp, but her jaw had begun to stiffen. Her mouth, even in death, wore a faint pout that reminded Dunn of his sister. Nearby on the floor was the Charter Arms.

"Done with your pictures over here?" Dunn asked Myles.

The younger man nodded. "Don't tell me you want prints," Myles asked.

"Yes, prints. I want prints. Including this," he said, sticking his pen carefully through the trigger guard and moving the weapon to the desk. The gun was blue steel. Two chambers appeared to have been fired.

Myles made some huffy noises, largely at the implied questioning of his diagnosis of the situation. Finally: "Looks a little like your sister, doesn't she?"

Dunn shuddered. He turned to assess the clutter on the girl's desk. The suicide note was still in the typewriter, black and crisp, brief and unadorned. The statement apologized to those she had hurt, it referred to pain she could no longer bear. It was signed, *With love, Moira.* Fairly impersonal. Dunn had seen notes that rambled for twenty pages. He had pulled notes off floppy disks. Notes as terse as *DONT CALL,* notes that ended with *This is Raymond, signing off.* He reread Moira's last words, then glanced around the room, looking for corroboration. And looking for a second bullet.

The house, built around the turn of the century, had undergone extensive renovations in the decade that had passed since Horace Pealey's death. Conversion into a two-family rental property had criminally disfigured the once noble Victorian into a utilitarian but obscene hodgepodge of separate entrances, aluminum storm windows, and makeshift interior walls. Moira's living room looked like it had once been a parlor of some majesty.

Now it was sentenced to mediocrity, its dignity transformed to gloom. The walls were an annoying shade of
blue; the pieces—or set, as they wanted to be called—were
classic Levitz, matching and looking still under warranty,
perhaps not even paid off. Except for some pictures cut
from magazines and pathetically taped to the wall, Moira
Doheny was the only decoration.

On a stool next to the TV was a purse. Dunn opened it
carefully and pulled out the wallet. The deceased had been
twenty-two years old, five feet four inches, did not require
glasses, could not drive a semi. The license was due to
expire three months after the driver had. The Registry
camera had cast its usual unsavory pallor over her face,
and had ferreted out the most minor of complexion diffi-
culties, turning small beauty emergencies into capital of-
fenses. The detective keyed his radio and called in Moira's
number for state and local queries. He looked back at her
face.

Gabe Dunn's sister Rachel was about four years older
than this woman. Dunn had had the unwelcome task of
taking over a good part of her upbringing when he was a
teenager, at an age where sisters were still more of a liabil-
ity than an asset, a state they revert to now and then even
in adult life. He had always assumed that her pout came
from being the spoiled younger sister of three put-upon
brothers. All his life he had given her a hard time about it.
Dunn supposed that at the moment Moira Doheny had
good enough reason to pout.

Continuing his tour, the detective studied the ceiling
and walls until he located the bullet hole about three feet
up from the floor in the corner by the window. Chips of
the revolting blue gypsum dusted the rug below. He squatted down and poked at the hole cautiously with his pen.
The projectile had gone straight through the wallboard.
Peering in, he could see no daylight. Dunn stood up and

frowned at Myles, who sighed and reloaded his camera. "I don't like this. Ballistics coming, you said?" Dunn asked.

Myles growled. "Yeah. Said he was on his way. We'll be here all fucking day."

Dunn's radio sputtered for a moment, then spat out, "Control to thirty-three." Thirty-three was the designation for the gray, unmarked Ford LTD Crown Victoria and the detectives it contained. When Dunn answered, the voice on the radio confirmed Moira's name and address, and her unsullied record. No one wanted her. Dunn put in a repeat request for the state ballistician.

"We're gonna miss *Cops,*" Myles said.

Dunn went through the rest of the apartment, checking the medicine cabinet, recent mail, desk drawers, the contents of her refrigerator. Moira had food-shopped recently. Above the kitchen sink, jars of cloudy water occupied the sunny end of the windowsill. An avocado seed pierced with toothpicks sat in one; the rest held carrot tops in various mysterious manifestations.

Moira's medicine chest held a dozen small plastic containers attesting to her pain. The detective located a clothbound address book in the bedroom. Inside the front cover there was a work number for "Dad." Unfortunately, she hadn't needed to write down her father's home address and phone.

At the foot of Moira's bed sat a small hope chest, presumably for holding the victim's small hopes. Dunn moved a sweat shirt and hairbrush, squatted down and lifted the lid. Rummaging through it, the detective found a bicycle lock, a stack of old bank statements, some clothes, a forgotten coupon organizer, magazine clippings ranging from "How to Balance your Checkbook" to "Thirty-day Makeover." The complexities of life seemed to have crowded out the hopes. A lot of those coupons had probably expired.

Back in the living room, the center desk drawer surrendered up a box of loose .38 shells. A conglomeration of various brands: Remington, Federal, some no-name discount stuff. Some practice rounds in disposable aluminum casings. Still sufficiently lethal.

Finally the beat man's voice from the front porch heralded the arrival of the medical examiner. Dr. Gloria Mei, all fifty-nine inches of her, would soon put to rest any doubts as to Moira Doheny's status. She entered the living room slightly out of breath, as if the effort of maintaining even those fifty-nine inches of stature among a forest of Goliaths was an ongoing exertion.

"Hello, boys, what have we got?" Heads turned to look down on her. "My, my, my," she continued, setting down her bag. She looked around at the boys like they were somehow responsible for this travesty.

While she poked and prodded, Dunn went to the side window and pushed aside the curtain. The window overlooked the rear of the Store 24, which occupied the corner of North and Moody streets. January's low afternoon sun cast long shadows on the sidewalk. Dunn couldn't help noticing that the sky had never been more cloudless. The visibility was unlimited and the wind calm. He knew in his heart that this day would have been the day he finally soloed. Republic Aviation was one of those old-fashioned flight schools that still cut your shirt off, nailing it to the office wall with the date etched on the front with a Marks-A-Lot. Dunn was wearing the expendable T-shirt he had optimistically pulled on that morning. The front had grease stains and holes. The original inscription on the back, thankfully, wouldn't have shown, pinned to the wall.

Dr. Mei checked the temperatures both of Moira Doheny and her living room. She confirmed the absence of an exit hole. No other wounds, signs of struggle, or assault. Pupils were normal and even. Dunn sat down on the edge of the couch and watched as she worked. Finally, she stood up, removed her latex gloves, and repacked her bag. The detective pulled out a small notebook.

"OK," she began. "Single bullet wound, death looks sudden. From the stippling around the wound, I'd say it was very close range, almost contact. Everything else, negative. Lividity suggests the blood settled with the body in this position. Rigor's just starting. Could suggest six to eight hours. That's corroborated by her temperature. Ninety-one degrees. With this room temperature, we could pretty much say seven hours. Seven degrees, seven hours. An hour each way."

She sounded like a miniature Julia Child. Seven degrees, seven hours. A slow oven. Just a pinch of powder burns. She smiled down at Dunn. He was waiting for the wine recommendation.

"Gloria, can we get an autopsy?" he asked.

"On what grounds?" she asked. Suicides were no longer routinely done since the last cutbacks. On the other hand, if anything turned up later, they all had asses to cover.

"You need more than gut feeling, right?"

"I need more than gut feeling," she said. "A bit more."

"How about trajectory of the bullet?"

She started to unlatch her bag again. "I can probe it for you here, if there's any question."

Dunn thought for a moment. "The note mentions pain. From the looks of her medicine cabinet she could have been referring to physical pain. We can see what her doctor says, if he's willing to talk to us. We can find out what the prescriptions were for. But if she was hurting enough to kill herself, that would be useful to try to confirm."

Dr. Mei laughed. "What do you think we'll find? A sledgehammer in her frontal lobe?"

"I don't know. Some kinds of pain would be detectable, wouldn't they? You didn't say you needed a great reason."

She seemed unconvinced. Dunn added: "OK, how about this? She had all that stuff in her medicine cabinet, enough to put her to sleep forever. Women prefer that method. Why'd she pick a gun?"

She frowned and bent down to retrieve her bag. "All right. You got your post. I'm releasing the scene. Can I use the phone?"

"I'd rather you didn't," Dunn said.

"You really believe it's not suicide," she said, looking at him. "What's bothering you?"

Dunn shrugged. "It'll be your call, Gloria. But look around this room. Look in the kitchen, in the sink. Look all over. The clutter. The laundry, dirty dishes. All within normal limits. Do you see despair here? Unless she despaired of ever paying off the furniture."

"She didn't shoot herself out of despair. She shot herself because of the pain, remember?"

"Did she? That's what we need to find out. That's why we need the autopsy," Dunn answered.

"We know she took painkillers. What's really bothering you, Gabe?"

Dunn walked her to the front door. The beat officer was leaning against the wall, carrying on a conversation with his radio.

"The second bullet," he answered. "Use my car phone. It's the gray Crown Vic, right out front."

Tremors continued to travel through Chris Alexei's limbs like aftershocks. His body still felt the effects from the night in an unheated jail cell. But Moira hadn't helped. She definitely hadn't helped. He was unclear whether the spasms were a physical response, or an avalanche of emotions, unbidden and unfamiliar. "Let's drive by again," he suggested out loud.

"Are you out of your fucking mind?" Chris's partner,

Eugene Sollors, had just shelled out a thousand dollars to make bail for Chris. He felt responsible for Chris until his Monday-morning arraignment. Eugene wanted to protect his investment. The two were sitting together in Eugene's car, parked near the pond at Greenlawn Cemetery. No one around to bother them but ducks and ghosts.

"OK, just down North Street. We can see from there."

At twenty-seven, Eugene was older and wiser by two years. At least when it came to handling people, dead or alive. When it came to handling the inanimate portion of the universe he deferred to Chris's proven superiority. Wires, locks, cars, buildings. Stone, metal, electricity, air, fire, and wind. Chris was master of all. But the kid didn't know jack shit about people.

"Chris, they'll find her. Her sister will come by. Someone will come by." Patience was as foreign to Eugene as emotions were to Chris. Death hands us strange scripts.

Chris scowled. He had loved Moira. Off and on. He didn't like the thought of her rotting on the floor of her apartment.

His partner changed the subject. "Look, man, what do you wanna do about the cards? Go through them now? Divide them up?"

Chris looked blankly at the box of cards. Most were in plastic sleeves or heavy protectors, each one bearing a small Sports King price tag. Eugene's timing left him derailed.

Eugene pulled the box toward him and scooped out some of the contents. *1962 Topps, 1963 Fleer, Near Mint. Hank Aaron, Willie Mays, $150 each. Rookie Parade Catchers, $125. Jimmy Piersall, $2.50, Billy O'Dell, $6. Number 423: Rival League Relief Aces, 5 bucks.*

"How ya wanna do this?" Eugene asked.

Number 312: Colt .45's Team. 9 bucks.

* * *

The landlord's name was Haynes. He had rented the downstairs apartment to Moira about a year earlier. She had been a fairly quiet tenant except when various and sundry boyfriends showed up. Sometimes all at once. Mr. Haynes couldn't figure it out. But luckily the couple upstairs, in whose kitchen he now sat, were hard of hearing. So he hadn't had to take any action. She paid her rent on time, kept the place clean. Dunn asked the couple what, if anything, they had heard or seen in the last twenty-four hours. They had heard and seen nothing. Not surprisingly Dunn had had to repeat the question four times.

The detective asked the landlord to show him everything he had touched in Moira's apartment. The two filed back downstairs and out onto the porch. Scattered along the sidewalk, the onlookers seemed settled in for the duration.

"What did you do when you first arrived, Mr. Haynes?"

The landlord turned and faced the separate entrance to Number Two Moody Street. Fighting off the distracting sounds of police radios and the chatter of the audience, he put one hand to his forehead and concentrated on the task. Finally, he stepped forward.

"I rung the bell." He reached out and extended a finger to within an eighth of an inch of the square plastic buzzer. "I rung several times, in case they're in, you know, I don't wanna surprise them." Then he groped for his key ring and pulled it out. "There was no answer, so I let myself in. She had a problem with a drain in the bathroom. That's what I come for."

"When did you talk to her about it?" Dunn asked. "Did she know you were coming?"

"Today's Saturday? Thursday, I guess. She called me Thursday. I told her I'd try to get to it this weekend. I like to take care of things as soon as possible."

Dunn looked skeptical. "Was it the first time she called about the drain?"

"Well, the first time where it was this bad," he explained a bit defensively.

Dunn pushed open the door. "What next?"

Mr. Haynes stepped into Moira's hallway. The living room was off to the left. Down the hall to the right was the door to the kitchen. A small closet was carved into the space below what would be the entry stairwell to the upstairs apartment. He stopped and looked down at his feet. "There was mail. I was stepping on her mail. I picked it up, I put it on the radiator."

He pointed to a peeling radiator next to the doorway to the kitchen, where the mail had lain until Dunn had thrown it into the evidence file. Then he continued slowly down the hall, treading deliberately, as if walking through a choreographed routine.

Dunn looked after him in surprise. They had passed the open door to the living room. "You didn't go in here?" he asked, thumb extended.

Mr. Haynes shook his head. "Not till afterward."

"After what?"

"After I fixed the drain. Didn't take long. I snaked it, and poured in some Liquid Plumr for good measure."

"You fixed the drain?" Dunn asked incredulously. Moira's bloody corpse just inside the open door, the desk lamp illuminating her last declaration. And Mr. Haynes had walked right by, no, scooped up the mail a foot from the doorway, then walked by. Dunn backed up a step, looked into the living room, and noted the position of the body, now covered with an orange, ribbed bedspread. The top of her head would have been visible. Her flaming red hair against the forest-green carpet. Green, which looks so good with red hair. Dunn shook his head. "You fixed the drain," he repeated, rhetorically this time.

"Snaked it," said Mr. Haynes.

We should all have landlords that efficient.

After mucking about in the bathroom sufficiently to ob-
literate any useful clues, Mr. Haynes had gone back the
way he had come, this time poking his head in each room,
presumably just to snoop. The scene awaiting him in the
living room had not escaped him this time. Mr. Haynes
had found his way backward out the front door, set his tool
box down on the porch, and leaned on the buzzer for
Number Four. At one thirty-four P.M. the Salem Police Department took the call.

Clarence Doheny had sent the kid back to Allied Lumber to get another few pounds of eight-penny nails before
it closed. Working on Saturdays was a rarity, but this customer was in a hurry. The basement of the modest Witch-
craft Heights garrison was looking less like a boiler room
and more like a family room, whatever the hell that was.
Doheny had built dozens of family rooms without ever
seeing the need to own one. The room you curled up in
when you had a living room you were afraid to sit in. Or
where you stuffed all the junk that couldn't take the heat
up in the attic. But not for long. People who built family
rooms invariably went out and bought pool tables.

Doheny wore a "This Old House" T-shirt and a six-foot-
three frame, useful for putting up blue board. He had been
whistling "auld lang syne" under his breath for the past
four days. Like a shred of food stuck between his teeth, it
refused to dislodge.

From somewhere above him Doheny heard a phone
ring. He slid another four-by-eight sheet of plywood into
position on the floor frame. The next piece would need to
be cut down.

"Hey, mister, uh, telephone" came the distant voice of
one of the garrison's younger occupants. Doheny brushed
off his hands and headed up the basement steps. When he
emerged into the warm kitchen, he took the receiver from

the teenager with a look of impatience. Probably Allied verifying the charge.

"Yeah? Clarence Doheny here."

It wasn't the lumber company.

"Moira's dead" came the voice.

The ballistician had cut open the wall, marked the trajectory, and retrieved the bullet. Looked about right for the Charter Arms, but time would tell. Lots of time, the state's specialty. His unofficial pronouncement was that the bullet had been angling slightly upward when it hit the wall. It had mushroomed somewhat in the soft decaying wood. A high quality, jacketed hollow-point load. A good police bullet.

"Why would a suicide shoot at the wall first?" asked Dunn, knowing that the ballistician was no psychologist but had seen far more victims shot by their own hands than had Dunn.

"It's not unheard of. Just trying out the gun sometimes."

"Like hesitation cuts before they slit their wrists," Dunn mused.

"I guess. Not my department, cuts." The man rummaged around in his tool kit. He continued: "If she fired from that chair, I'd say it was about lap level. No higher." Myles had finished photographing the bullet and handed it back to him.

"Could it have fired again when it dropped, or as she was falling?" asked Dunn.

"Not this gun." The ballistician, whose name was MacKenzie, went to work dusting the Charter Arms. On the frame above the grip he lifted a partial. Nothing else useful. Good prints off guns are difficult to obtain.

"Do me a favor while you're here, Sam," said Dunn. "Could you check her fingers . . . see if the print's hers?"

MacKenzie hesitated, bagging the gun.

"I'm feeling a little hinky about this case," explained Dunn. "No one particular thing, just somehow the picture is out of focus. Doesn't smell right. Doesn't ring true."

Overpowered by the detective's metaphors, MacKenzie picked up his single glass slide and bent down to pull up Moira's right arm. The print had been on the left side of the gun. Dunn slipped the bag and rubber band off her hand and directed his flashlight on the fingertips. MacKenzie studied the thumb, the logical candidate.

"Looks like hers," he announced. The girl would be fingerprinted at the autopsy. They could make an official comparison then. He carefully replaced the bag, resecuring it with the rubber band around the wrist.

Ballistician and booty departed for 1010 Commonwealth Avenue, home of the state lab in Boston. Moira's body was removed and heading for Salem Hospital. As he locked up, Dunn looked at his watch. Scene secured at three-forty. Jake could still catch *Cops.*

Chapter 2

Family Affair

It had been exactly one week since Detective Billy Trinidad had rotated his Steelcase desk ninety degrees, breaking with a tradition of parallel desks in the Criminal Investigation Division since back when they were still arresting witches. Billy Trinidad, who doubled as the evidence officer and possessed one of the only two keys to the drug vault, now sat with his back to the window and faced the door, startling all who entered. Jake Myles had been the first postrotation entrant and had asked who the new receptionist was. The epitaph was dying hard.

Dunn piled an assortment of directories on his own parallel desk and began looking up the identity of Moira's father from his phone number. Myles had stopped off downstairs to run some of the names in the girl's address book. When he strode in moments later with the first of the printouts, he paused and bent over Trinidad's desk. Trinidad had come in for the Saturday four-to-midnight shift. "Any messages?" Myles asked sweetly.

The reverse directory for Beverly-Lynn-Peabody-Salem listed the number as belonging to Becker and Doheny General Contracting, Inc., on Highland Avenue in Salem. Dunn jotted down the address and stood up. "OK. First order of business is, we talk to the girl's family. Then we check with her neighbors, the store next door, friends in her book. Any juicy history?" he asked Myles, indicating the printouts.

"Nothing earthshaking. Why are you treating this as a homicide?" Myles asked.

"Every death's a homicide until we prove otherwise," Dunn answered.

"Save that for the press. *Why* are you treating it as a homicide, Gabe? How much proof do you need?"

Dunn shook his head. "It's too perfect. The note, the gun with her prints, powder burns. Could be a clever killer."

"All that stuff—that's called *evidence.* You've been spending too much time at the Loew's Cinema. This is *life.* This is *Salem.* Killers here are not rocket scientists."

"So how come half our murders go unsolved?"

"Only 'cause we ain't either," Myles stated.

Remembering his T-shirt and the somber nature of their errand, Dunn asked Trinidad if there were any clean shirts around he could borrow. He didn't bother asking Myles, whose shirts all looked like they originated from the Honolulu Airport Gift Shop. Trinidad fished around in a large brown evidence bag under his desk and tossed Dunn a dark-blue wad.

"What body is this from?" asked Dunn, holding up a wrinkled polo shirt that otherwise passably matched his lanky frame.

"It's mine. Just give it a good shake."

Dunn removed the torn T-shirt he had hoped with luck and calm winds to lose that day. He started to stuff it into his bottom desk drawer, but Myles caught sight of the back.

" 'Nobody's Ugly at 2 A.M.' I gotta have this shirt!"

Dunn threw it at him. Pulling on the polo shirt, he said: "Let's go see the father."

* * *

When the question of suicide came up, the family members were quiet. Moira's sister Sasha had joined her father with a baby in tow before Dunn and Myles arrived. The landlord had notified her. She in turn had called her father. Both the Dohenys were still noticeably in shock. Neither had known of the decedent's prior whereabouts or plans. Neither raised any argument to the suggestion that Moira had taken her own life.

"She got these headaches a lot," explained Sasha, clutching the small, sticky child on her lap. The woman was in her mid-twenties, auburn hair pulled back with a pair of silver barrettes. Freckled skin that rivaled her sister's, and an Irish face that mirrored her father's. "Moira was in a car accident last spring. She had some sort of head injury. She was unconscious for a while, and then later started getting these pains. Sometimes her pills helped, sometimes they didn't. Sort of like bad migraines, only worse, she used to tell me."

Dunn looked at her father. Mr. Doheny cleared his throat, then added in a strangely modulated voice: "Check with her doctor. He had a name for it. 'Chronic post something syndrome.' I got a brother living with chronic pain, too. Terrible thing. And then her. And now this . . ."

"Did she ever talk of suicide?" Dunn asked. The detectives spoke in tones low and hushed, as if someone were asleep at their feet.

They both shook their heads. But still no protestations.

"Did either of you see or hear from her the last couple of days?" Negative, again. Sasha indicated she had not been home the previous night, so didn't know if her sister had tried to reach her.

"Anything else bothering her besides the headaches? Money problems, boyfriend problems?" asked Dunn.

The whole family had money problems, as it turned out. Mr. Doheny had nothing lined up after the boiler-room make-over. Sasha was out of work. Her live-in boyfriend sold flavored popcorn from a pushcart in the Liberty Tree Mall. That plus her unemployment checks soon would be insufficient to stop the bank from repossessing her car. Without her car, job opportunities had a way of shriveling up.

"Moira and me, we helped each other a lot recently. You know, back and forth. I had cash when she needed it for medical expenses. She hasn't been able to repay it yet. That bothered her, I know. I told her not to worry about it. But, like I'm losing the car, and she knew how that is, since hers was totaled in the accident. It's a real drag."

Dunn glanced at Myles. He reached into his jacket for the address book and turned again to the pair.

"Would either of you recognize any of the names in here, especially the ones on the first page? They seemed to be important to her." Dunn handed the book to Mr. Doheny. Sasha looked over her father's shoulder. The baby, who looked about seven months, reached out to feel the cover.

The names inside the cover and on the first page, the page before the A's, weren't in order. Most were just first names or family members: *Dad—work, Adele, Sasha, Mom —Calif, Mr. Haynes, Saratoga (main), S's ext:, Chris, BCN mystery riff, Dr. Byfield, Eugenes, CVS (pharm)*. The random category seemed to spill over into the A's as well. *Dominos, J G, cable TV.*

Moira's father looked up and shrugged helplessly. "Sasha, that's her sister." He pointed at his daughter. "And her mom. Moved to Long Beach three or four years ago. These others . . ." He looked pained. When your child starts acquiring friends you don't know, a life you don't know, well, the next thing you know they go and get themselves killed.

Sasha looked up. "Byfield's her doctor, Dad." To Dunn:

"Adele, I think her last name is Prego, or Predo, or something. A friend. Used to be close. And Chris, she was going with him off and on. Eugene sounds familiar. Someone in Chris's crowd was named Eugene. I don't know about Eugene*s.*"

Dunn studied the page upside down. "Could be Eugene S. Do you know Eugene's last name? Or Chris's?"

Negative on both. *J G* had two numbers. The old one, crossed off, was a Lynn exchange. The second was Beverly.

"Can you tell me anything about these guys? Did Moira talk about them at all?" Dunn asked.

Sasha glanced at her father. "I think one or the other had been in some sort of trouble. It wasn't a particularly good crowd."

"Trouble with the law? Any idea what it was?"

Sasha shook her head. Dunn got a sense she felt she had to protect her sister. Or someone else. "Moira was . . . well, dumb sometimes. She kept picking up strays, thinking she could change them."

"What about Moira herself? Was she ever involved? Was she ever in trouble?" Dunn asked.

"No. Moira wasn't that type."

Myles leaned forward and cleared his throat. "Was she the type who could commit suicide?" he asked.

Sasha paused. "She kept talking about . . . escape."

"Escape? From what?" Myles continued.

" 'Gotta do something about my life,' she told me."

"You think ending it was what she had in mind?"

"I don't know, Officer."

Dunn had made a copy of the note found on Moira's desk. He handed it to the pair and watched them as they read it.

" 'The only way out?' " Mr. Doheny gave a low moan. "No, sugar, *not* the only way out. Not the only way," he repeated over and over, fighting for his voice.

Dunn glanced at Sasha, who was shaking her head. "Is that Moira?" he asked. "Did your sister write that?" he asked quietly.

Sasha shifted her hold on the child and looked up. "Not the kid I grew up with. But you know, the pain really changed her." She couldn't speak after that. Instead, with her free hand she held the paper up to her face and inhaled deeply. It didn't smell of Moira. It smelled of death.

Dunn looked at notes like that and thought of the souls who wrote them, the words almost more shocking than the act itself. Putting it on paper avoids argument. Buck stops here. Pen runs dry. No further discussion. If they could be stopped mid-sentence, stopped from writing the scene they then felt compelled to play out, could they be saved? After over thirteen years on the force, Dunn still didn't know. The more he tried to understand suicides, the less he understood about everything else.

Thirteen years a cop. Nearly nine years a detective, five a sergeant. Student pilot for almost two. Five and a half years since his piano was last tuned; divorced four years; two years, one month, four days since his last cigarette. His left knee, injured in a chase two years previously, still bothered him. He wasn't improving at bat. A few of the hairs which topped his five-foot-ten-inch frame were no longer the color of straw. Cops age earlier than the rest of the world.

Dunn supposed that every day you didn't have strong enough reason to die, you kept on living.

Chapter 3

Leslie's Retreat

Eugene Sollors flipped off the top of a Rolling Rock and handed the bottle to Chris. "You sure it was Judd ratted you out?" Sollors's arms were tanned, his motions expansive.

"Course it was. He drove Wednesday night. No one else had the kind of information he had. Hell, there wasn't even that much in the safe." He took a long swallow of beer. Dark-haired, wiry, Chris Alexei was a safe man. One of the best on the North Shore. He specialized in square doors and alarm systems. Mostly the brute force method where you cut the wires and go away for an hour. If no one answered, the place was yours. You could peel the safe at your leisure.

Round doors were tougher. Usually beyond the capability of his crowbar. But Thursday night the Sports King had had a round door and it had eventually yielded. Eugene was with him on that job and had said it would be worth the effort. Chris didn't like to deal in merchandise anymore. Fucking waste of time. But Eugene knew baseball cards. He was a collector himself, a little sideline. Eugene knew which ones were good. And he claimed they would be untraceable, easy to get rid of. Sell a few a week. Piece of cake.

Judd Grimes had turned Chris in for a liquor store B&E

that had netted them only a few hundred in cash and some lottery tickets. Judd had no part in the Sports King job the following night, thank God. Chris and Eugene reaped over eighty thousand dollars worth of cards, plus what cash was in the safe. Bail would have been considerably higher if the police had known about that one.

Ill at ease, Chris tapped on his bottle. "The dickhead. I haven't used him in a long time, you know. Shoulda known better. He's strung out, or high, or dope sick or something half the time. He's been doing smash and grabs and getting caught. Too much snow. He's too easy to crack. He thinks he's such a hot-shit wheelman. Fucker's never driving for me again."

Partners, your so-called "friends," are your weakest link when you're competent. You go to all the trouble of avoiding prints, tracks, finding the VCR in stores with cameras and pulling the tapes, you don't leave tools or calling cards behind, you don't crap on the floor. You're a professional. Then your buddy gets picked up by the cops and replays the tape in his head.

"So you wanna do something about him? I'll take care of him. Bang him out before he leaves town or something."

Chris made a face. "Later, maybe. He's almost not worth the effort. I got other things on my mind. When'd you get the message they popped me?"

"Adele told me this morning. I came right down, Chris."

"This morning? I called nine or ten last night. I told her to get ahold of you right away."

"Well, I did a job last night, OK? She was asleep when I got back. I didn't hear till eight this morning."

Bitch. "She coulda left you a fucking note. I had to spend all night in that shit house. That's the worst lockup I've ever . . ."

Eugene got up. "All right, you're out, OK? What'd they say about your liquor store job? Did you work a deal?"

". . . fucking *rat* in my cell. Miracle *he* was alive, 'cause it was cold as a bastard. Toilet stopped up. Cement bed . . ."

Eugene interrupted: "Chris, for chrissake, did you talk to them or what?"

". . . plexiglass over the bars so's you can't hang yourself it's so bad. No, asshole, I didn't give them your name, I didn't give them any other jobs. All they got is Cosgroves. Me and Judd. Lay off me."

While Myles checked with Moira's neighbors on Moody Street, Dunn tried tracking down her friends. None of the numbers under Chris and Eugene were listed in the reverse directory. The detective made a note to talk to a friend at the phone company on Monday. Tracking down the owners of unlisted and unpublished numbers was a pain in the butt. Required a court subpoena if you didn't have a little connection in the business office.

Adele's number was listed under Adele Prada, residing on Upham Street in North Salem, a few short blocks from Moody. Dunn gave it a try, but got no answer.

Next, he called the manager of the Store 24 to find out who might have been working when the girl died. Dunn had met the manager a couple of times. Hank Terrell lived down in the Willows section of Salem. Nice guy, cooperative. Terrell remembered Moira. Came into the store any and all hours. He gave Dunn the name and number of the midnight shift man.

Dunn called Archie Block and learned that Moira had in fact been in just after midnight Friday night, early Saturday morning. He couldn't remember exactly what time, or what she bought. The detective called Terrell back and asked if he could pull the in-store videotapes for that day.

Dunn had worked on a robbery of the store once, and knew that Terrell kept good tapes. A lot of places had equipment they paid thousands of dollars for, but they pinched pennies by never replacing the tapes. Comes a holdup and the tape's all snowy.

Terrell's tape of the robbery last year could have won an award for artistic merit. First a guy walks up to the cashier wearing plaid pants and a Grateful Dead T-shirt. Buck teeth, scarred face, shaved head. Buys a package of hot dogs and a pack of Marlboros. Leaves the store.

Five minutes later, same tape, guy with a ski mask and shotgun walks in, leans over the counter and threatens the cashier. Plaid pants, Grateful Dead T-shirt, same height, same hands. Cleans out the till. Gun waving, he backs down aisle three and grabs a package of hot dog buns. Then he beats it. Perfect disguise.

The boys played the tape up in CID for weeks. Could have sold tickets.

Predominantly blue collar with pockets of exceptions, North Salem was the twenty-six-car beat, variously known as the milk run or the North Salem retirement community, not due to the age of the residents, but due to their penchant for quiet, law-abiding lives. Cops assigned to the twenty-six-car were considered to be in retirement. The ones that had requested twenty-six spent their nights on dinner breaks. The ones that hadn't spent their nights wondering what they had done wrong. Those who actually craved action crossed the river each night to back up somebody else.

North Salem is divided from the rest of the city by the North River and tidal canal. To the west it abuts the city of Peabody; to the north the Danvers River flows into Beverly Harbor. Nearly three-quarters of its acreage is given to cemeteries, parks, and golf course. Much of the ward's

tranquility is attributable to the bulk of its population being either dead or golfing. The remaining four thousand or
so, mostly Democrats of diverse ethnicity, occupy an architectural spectrum of structures in an area bisected by
Route 114, one of about three major but inadequate traffic
routes into town. Route 114 is called North Street when it
enters Salem, and, lined with small neighborhood shops
and wooden houses, it crosses the river and dumps its con-
voy at the corner of the McIntire historic district downtown. Over three hundred years ago this road connected
the former municipalities of Salem Village and Salem
Town. By the time the latter became known as Danvers,
farms had given way to a dense leather industry, with all
the supporting manufacturers and suppliers it required.

Dunn had spent much of his youth in North Salem. His
grandfather had worked in the tanneries, and raised a family in the shadow and stench of the factories. In the days
prior to zoning, these stood shoulder to shoulder with the
houses of workers, dumping acids and heavy metals into
the river and untold hazards into the air. In the heyday of
the leather industry, the noise, the fumes and smoke were
the sound and smell of jobs. North Salem's lifeblood, now
its poison, lies deeply embedded in the bottom of the canal.

Not as tight a neighborhood as some, the area still had
plenty of places for kids to hang out and trespass as the
need arose. Besides Mack Park and the cemeteries, there
were abandoned cars down by the river, and, behind one
of the remaining leather factories on Buffum Street, piles
of leather scraps to lie on. There was Sargent Street, iso-
lated, tree-shrouded, for parking with girls or bottles or
both.

North Salem had not always been so law-abiding, nor
was Moira Doheny's blood the first blood shed here. In the
1830s homes in the neighborhood became stations along

the underground railway as slaves from the South made their treacherous way to Canada. Some sixty years earlier, Lieutenant Colonel Alexander Leslie was turned back at the bridge in the earliest known resistance by the colonists, thwarting the British efforts to uncover munitions hidden in the North fields. The unofficial monument to that illustrious event is a local pub near the bridge called Leslie's Retreat. To the current citizenry who breakfast there, to the sons and daughters of those who resisted in 1775, the first blood spilled in the Revolutionary War was Salem blood.

Chapter 4

The Policeman's Lot

Detective Daniel Braedon was staring glumly at his pocket calendar. "I wait six weeks to get the weekend off and we land a homicide." Moira's address book lay open before him, turned to "D-E-F."

Dunn looked up at him. "It's not officially a homicide, Danny. But Jake and I have the autopsy in a half hour, and he's looking at the Store 24 tapes. Billy's in, too. He's on a B and E. Sheila's off. I need you to be making these calls, buddy. We got all kinds of stuff happening."

"Sheila's *off?* How about me? *I'm* fucking off!"

"You want to find her? Be my guest. Only make the calls first."

"We were going skiing. Car was all packed when you called. I told her we should've left early. Weekend's half over by the time she decides what clothes to bring. And by then she don't need any. My next shot, it'll be fucking spring. Six goddamn weeks."

"We woulda beeped you. You can run, Daniel, but you cannot hide. Anyway, it's seven weeks," Dunn informed him.

"What's seven weeks?"

"Your next weekend off." Dunn had gone back to his report. One of the few detectives to avoid the word processor out of some vague, unknowable primitive fear, he

38

wrote each word carefully in block, capital letters, giving his Officer's Reports a look somewhere between urgency and adolescence. Sticking to all caps avoided the whole issue of capitalization. It was also easier for the mildly dyslexic writer to get the words right. Dyslexia sufficient to ensure that reading and writing would never come easily to the man. Studying for his sergeant's exam seven years ago had been a grim reminder that he had not entirely over-come the disability. Yet he had made it. The day he got his promotion, anonymous members of the department plas-tered a **DYSLEXICS UNTIE** banner on his bulletin board. It was three days before he figured it out.

Dunn signed and dated his report. Braedon was still studying him from three desks away. "What are you talk-ing about? They always told me six weeks. I work four days, I'm off two, that's a six-day week."

"Your days off move back one day a week. Trust me. It takes seven days to get back to the full weekend. That's seven weeks, lapper."

"They explained it, my first day back is actually the sev-enth day. So I work five out of seven days . . ."

"Forget that crap. That has nothing to do with it. Half of what they tell you has nothing to do with anything."

Braedon was very quiet. After a while he said: "You may have something there, Gabe. I think I've been given bad information."

"Just take a look at your calendar. Count the weeks yourself."

Braedon looked at the month of January, then turned to February, then March. After a few minutes he looked back up at Dunn. "They've been screwing me. For eight years they've been screwing me."

Dunn grinned at him. He rolled back his chair, walked to Braedon's desk, and tapped the address book. "Call

these people, will you, Danny? Gunstock will still have
snow in the spring. They'll make it for you specially."

Dunn's trouble had been the middles of words. He'd
nail the beginning, the ending, stare at it and the sucker
would look complete. But the middle would have leaked
out like a liquid-center cherry. *Decedent* still occasionally
came out *decent,* and sometimes *descant* on some of his
reports. Myles would read them out loud and suddenly
burst into song, usually the high-soprano part of "America
the Beautiful."

Chapter 5

Walk on the Wild Side

Moira's father came down to the hospital morgue later Saturday night to make positive identification prior to the autopsy. Myles met him in the hallway and took him inside. Dr. Mei raised the covering from the girl's face. She glanced up at Mr. Doheny. He began to shake. "That's my little girl," he whispered.

Myles led him back out to the corridor and gave him a cigarette. "She always got after me to quit, you know. I told her when she gave up running with thieves I'd give up smoking."

"Do you need a ride home, Mr. Doheny?" Myles asked.

"No, thanks. I've got the truck. What happens to her now? When they're done in there?" he asked, controlling his voice with difficulty.

"The medical examiner will probably release the body first thing in the morning. You can make your arrangements for then."

Mr. Doheny looked back at the door to the morgue. "How long will it take?"

"The post-mortem? An hour or two," Myles said.

"Maybe I should wait . . ."

This is no operation; she won't be going to no Recovery . . .

"That's not really necessary, Mr. Doheny. They won't be

41

able to tell you anything tonight. You want me to call Sasha?"

Mr. Doheny looked through Myles, to some point inches behind his head. "No, that's all right. I've got the truck . . ."

"Right."

On the way back from the autopsy, Dunn and Myles took a quick detour through the Point to check out what was happening on the street and to see if anyone would own up to shooting Moira Doheny.

The Point neighborhood of Salem was the twenty-two-car beat, the only two-man beat in the city. Despite recent efforts by law-abiding residents to take back what was, years ago, a quiet, respectable neighborhood, a great majority of the police log addresses nowadays were in the Point. Separating the area from the waters of the South River and Salem Harbor were industrial buildings, boatyards, and darkened, brick apartment houses, gutted by despair and drained of life. In the dim doorways of Ward and Harbor Streets, in the bright lights of Lafayette, you could get whatever you wanted and a lot of things you didn't want. On Saturday nights the detectives routinely rolled through the neighborhood once or twice in their familiar unmarked Ford Crown Victorias, making their presence known, checking out any new players, passing the time with the old.

For the regulars, almost all Saturday drug activity ceased between four and twelve when the night-shift detectives were on, except between nine and ten when they were known to return to the office to watch TV.

Most of the CID night detectives had worked the twenty-two beat when they were in uniform. Cops bid on twenty-two if they wanted to do police work and catch bad guys. The "real" section, they called it. They were the "real" police. They knew enough Spanish to say, *"Mantenga las manos visibles para mi."* The residents knew enough English to say "Get the fuck out of my apartment." They all understood each other pretty well.

Dunn and Myles made a quick circuit down Congress Street, then onto Palmer, finally turning back onto Lafayette. A group of familiar faces in front of the Lincoln Hotel spilled over the curb and out into the street. A couple of them were brawling. Breath hung in the air like steam. It was colder than a witch's tit. One of the faces waved down the car.

Myles lowered his window as he slowed the car. The frigid air smacked him in the face. "Hey, handsome," he said to the nearest man. A babble of greetings ushered forth. Several in the group had played against the Salem Police Department softball team once last summer. The civilian team called themselves *Las Antilles.* Every member had done time. The shortstop had narrowly escaped an assault charge two weeks earlier. Their pitcher had just finished three years of state time.

The detectives asked if anyone in the group had known Moira Doheny. Seemed an unlikely match, but Dunn had had stranger sources in his time. The name was passed around like an echo. No dice.

"Hey, Jake-man," yelled the pitcher. "When we gonna play again?"

"When you guys are ready to lose again. Where's the rest of your team?" Myles asked. The cops called them Las Enchiladas.

"Let's play tonight," said the shortstop.

"Gotta work, pal," Dunn responded, leaning over Myles. "Will you guys call me if you hear anything on this girl? She had a boyfriend, Chris something."

"Rematch! We wanna rematch! Anything—volleyball, wrestling, you name it, man," the shortstop persisted.

"How about a footrace?" Dunn suggested. Myles looked at his watch. *Cops* was starting in twenty minutes.

"A what???" said the shortstop.

"A race. Right now. All the way around the block. Me and you."

"Around the block? You suggesting a fucking *marathon,* man." The kid looked extremely doubtful.

"Come on! It'll get you in shape for the game. If you win, I'll pay you ten dollars," said Dunn.

"An' if you win?"

"We get to throw you in jail overnight," Myles answered.

The kid laughed and backed away. "I'm in bad shape, man."

Dunn rejoined: "Just one night. We promise you. It won't be so bad."

The shortstop turned back to his friends. "I gotta finish killing this man," he said over his shoulder. "An' you gonna miss your TV show."

"He's right," said Myles, who put the car in drive and began to crank up the window. "Hasta la eggroll," he yelled out to the group.

"I'll give you a head start," Dunn shouted through Myles's window.

"He's gotta kill the man," Myles explained, accelerating down Lafayette. "And we got our show."

At the New Derby Street intersection Myles pulled around a slow-moving Bronco towing a rowboat on a makeshift platform with wheels. "Get a real trailer," he hollered in annoyance.

Chapter 6

Ain't Got Long to Stay Here.

Saturday night just before nine, it started to snow. Chris lay down on his waterbed. One way to end an intolerable day is to go to bed. He had had no sleep the night before in the jail cell, and none all day. Not after having to deal with Moira. From where he lay, Chris watched the distracting white onslaught against his bedroom window. Visual white noise. Moira had been crying when he last held her here. Deep sobs coming from somewhere other than her head pain.

"I gotta get away from you, Chris," she had said. "I don't know if I can, but I gotta try."

"It bothers you now, what I do?"

She was quiet. Then she said: "I got used to the gifts. I got used to not asking where they came from, I guess. Not wondering, Chris. Not caring. But it's different now."

"Why is it different now?"

She didn't answer.

"What am I gonna do? Maybe be a phone company repair man? Take home a quarter what I do now. How are we gonna afford your medical bills? On your paychecks maybe?"

She rolled over and looked out the window. It was snowing that night, too. "I'm so cold. I think the cold makes the headaches worse. I think I'd be better off down South. I could live cheaper, too. Maybe Florida."

"Florida? *Jesus.*"

"*I want to see Universal Studios, you know? And Disney World. Always wanted to see that. It must be heaven living down there.*"

"*What am I gonna do in Florida, for chrissakes!*"

"*Yeah, it would be like going to heaven,*" she murmured, closing her eyes.

He rubbed her neck for a while. "*There's safes in Florida, I suppose.*"

"*Lie on the beach and eat all those oranges,*" she purred.

"*I'll get you oranges. All the oranges you want.*"

Then the pain started again. He could feel it in her neck. "*No, Chris. You can't come,*" she said in a faint voice. The stiffness gradually spread throughout her body. "*Oh, God, it hurts . . .*" She curled herself up into a fetal position and started to shake. "*I'm so cold,*" she said, choking on tears.

Chris wrapped himself around her and held her until she fell asleep.

At ten thirty-five Saturday night, a confidential source called in a not so anonymous tip. A Mom and Pop store on Boston Street next to the Peabody line was going to be hit. Sometime after midnight. The guy was certain and convincing enough to warrant a stakeout. Dunn hung up and swore. Myles was still watching TV.

"Hope you didn't have plans, Jake. We're gonna go watch a store."

Within a half hour they had picked a spot at the far side of a lot next door to the target. A few overnight parkers and a tree that intensified the darkness offered them some protection against discovery. Their view from the west was good. The thief would probably try the back door. The windows on the east side were too visible from the busy street.

The snow had stopped. The detectives unpacked their

coffees in the dark. Surveillances always began with some requisite grumbling. Dunn started them off this time.

"I was supposed to solo today. Instead I get a murder and this shit." He sighed.

Myles laughed. "You *wish* it was a murder. Why the hell couldn't he pick *this* place?" he said, pointing to the store whose lot they occupied, store and lot both located in the city of Peabody. The Peabody police would have owned the problem. Myles then switched to berating Christmas decorations, still in store windows, visible from where they sat.

"Jake, it's only January," Dunn retorted.

"They'll still be up in March. That's the thing about it." For Jake Myles, the mantle of police responsibility was a heavy one.

"Well, save your bitching for March."

Myles shut up for a minute. Then: "How're we gonna see anything if the snow starts up again? We'll be pretty obvious if we have the fucking wipers going all night."

Dunn answered: "Jake, let's not bleed until we're cut."

Finally, Myles was quiet for a while. Dunn thought about the autopsy, three hours earlier. The ballistician's first impression of the bullet they removed from Moira's head had been that the caliber looked right for the Charter Arms. No surprise there. Looked like one of the low-quality practice loads.

Death was due to the single bullet wound. The trajectory and powder burns were not inconsistent with firing at close range, and with the gun positioned in her right hand. The family had confirmed that the decedent had been right-handed.

Dr. Mei had found signs of the recent head injury. Moira's pain had been real. Toxicology results would take a couple weeks, however. The medical examiner could not find evidence of drugs or medication based on physical findings.

There had been some discussion over the manner of death. Dr. Mei was prepared to rule it a suicide, but one result of the examination had given Dunn a foothold. "It was one more complication," she had argued.

"It was a reason to live," Dunn had countered.

Dr. Mei had looked him in the eye. "All right, Gabriel. I'll mark it 'pending.' Get to work, young man."

Moira Doheny had been three months pregnant.

To the extent that thieving was seasonal work, winter was the season. More hours of darkness, and with some safes, your team needed all the dark you could get. Nearby windows would be tightly shut, and snow helped deaden any sounds. The disadvantage was with newly fallen snow. Then you had to deal with tracks.

Eugene Sollors was itching to go out. Not hit a difficult safe, Chris hadn't been in the mood to work. So it would have to be something simple that Eugene could do. He had been unlucky in netting a driver, though he had made a couple of calls. So he'd have to go it alone if he went out. The challenge and intoxication of breaking into a place nearly always beat whatever was on TV. Eugene was partying less than he had last year. He'd kicked his heroin habit, and spent his money instead in malls. Shopping could be as expensive a habit as drugs; you just switched your brand loyalties from Supertown to Magnavox.

But the snow was a pain. A better plan for the night might be to call up one of those chicken-shit wheelmen and go out for a few beers.

"He ain't coming," said Myles. It was nearly two A.M. They were cold and bored. Myles's cup was in a thousand small pieces. Dunn's was pierced through and through like a colander. Both had done this many, many times. That didn't make it particularly interesting anymore. They were each sick of the other's life and opinions.

"That's the fortieth time you've said that." A moment later, Dunn's beeper vibrated. He checked the number and picked up the car phone.

It was their informant. This particular thief had changed his mind and opted for a vacation day. Dunn thanked him for the update. "Screw this," he muttered and switched on the ignition.

Gabe Dunn's job with the force had taught him that life did indeed have a dark side. For him the best defenses were a deep and unyielding sense of humor to face it and total submersion in music to escape it. Sometimes. life's bright side was equally hard to face and required an even greater sense of humor. But through it all, tunes ran through his mind endlessly, as though his lifetime were an unending opera. Songs were the vessels of his emotions. Without melodies to define them, Dunn's reactions eluded and confused him.

The detective didn't play the piano well enough to keep his next-door neighbor from pounding on the wall. Dunn had never had lessons and rarely had a willing audience. What he did have in his favor was Roger, the neighbor's unregistered dog, forcing a sort of delicate truce between the two tenants. When Dunn crashed his way through the "Moonlight Sonata," the neighbor wouldn't call the land-lord. When Roger crapped on their walk, Dunn wouldn't call the dog officer. For three unregistered years he had tolerated the animal, watching it grow up from pup-pyhood. Dunn could remember when the turds were only the size of triple-A batteries.

The one time Dunn had spoken directly to Roger's owner was when he had apologized for a vigorous Chopin mazurka that had helped him recover from a big drug case he had lost in court.

"Chopin?" the guy answered from a crack in the door. "I thought it was *Slayer."* From behind the man, the dog barked. As the door slammed shut, Dunn yelled: "That's not a *dog* you've got in there, is it?"

Chapter 7

Roads Not Taken

Adele Prada woke up Sunday morning with the same recurring, crippling sensation she had had all week: the feeling she had ended up with the wrong guy.

When Chris had called Friday night from jail asking for Eugene and needing help, the sound of his voice had sent a wave through her body that had left her bewildered and agitated. Over the course of a few days her relatively contented existence had turned to one of discontent, settling rapidly into an abiding, bone-aching despair. She had known Chris for over four years. She had liked him at times, resented him at times, but had never loved him particularly. Before.

Except for his short temper, Eugene took pretty good care of her. Eugene had respect among their friends, his partners. Eugene always knew what to say, had the last word, the best joke. Adele had always considered tanned, strong Eugene to be better looking. But somehow, now, Chris's face held some newfound secret. Wolflike and mysterious, Chris had been transformed.

She was paralyzed, pinned to the bed with the weight of his image. Every cliché true, and every one of them inadequate. All other men were wretched for not being this one man.

She turned and gazed around the room. Eugene's stuff

was all over the place. A pair of his sneakers lay where he had dropped them last. These Nikes had carried him over rooftops, down fire escapes, away from cops. They had thrilled her with their essential maleness. Now they were pathetic. Like artificial feet. They didn't fool her anymore. How could Eugene know what a half-man he had become? His sudden diminishment choked her with something akin to profound pity.

The phone erupted by her ear. Adele recoiled for a moment in irritation, unable to leave where she was. Her arms were glued to the bed with her anguish. The rude intrusion was more than she could bear.

But it could be Chris.

Chris had given her the impression for four years that she, Adele, was not quite his type. He had taken no more than polite interest in her during the times they had all spent together, Eugene and Adele, Chris and Moira, then Chris and whoever, then back with Moira. Or Chris and Judd, or someone else, when they had a job to do. It wasn't for Adele that Chris came over. It was for everything but. One thing, though, now Moira was dead.

Moira Doheny was dead.

Adele shoved one hand back into reality and yanked the receiver to her ear. "Hello?"

"Is this Adele Prada?"

She wasn't seriously expecting it to be him, but the disappointment made her aware of how hard her heart was pounding. "That's me," she whispered with effort. Who the hell was this guy, another half-man.

"This is Detective Sergeant Gabe Dunn, Salem Police. We're investigating the death of Moira Doheny. I believe you were acquainted with her?"

"Yes, I heard." Adele cleared her throat, getting her voice to engage. She recognized her caller, though he clearly hadn't placed her. "She shot herself or something yesterday?"

"We haven't made a final determination. We would like to ask you a few questions if you don't mind. Would it be possible for us to drop by this morning?"

Adele looked at the clock. It was nine-fifteen. Eugene was supposed to come over later. God knows when. He had probably just gone to bed. "What time?"

"At your convenience."

"All right, OK. Give me like an hour?"

"We'll be there," Dunn said and hung up.

Adele dialed Eugene's apartment and left a warning on his answering machine. Then she got up to take a shower.

The hot water embraced and comforted her. *Grab hold of the reins, Adele,* she commanded, squeezing her eyes shut to force Chris's face from her mind. *Officer, Eugene and I were together all night. She was in a lot of pain. She was always in such pain. I wish I could have done something more for her. Moira shot herself. She shot herself. So sorry to hear . . . so sorry.*

No fresh, unsmudged prints had been found on the typewriter when Myles had fumed it. He had even checked the power switch. The machine now sat on the counter next to the copier in the detectives' office. For ten minutes Dunn stared at it from his seat. Her final words? Her last confidant? Somehow he didn't think so. They had removed and bagged the paper, and tested the typeface at the scene. It had compared positively with the note. Masquerading as Moira's oracle, this instrument of deceit had betrayed her. But Dunn knew that it would take a lot more than intuition to justify department time and money be spent on what even the girl's relatives had accepted as a suicide.

The black IBM Selectric, far better than the one the

CID had, was now ruined by the SuperGlue they used in the fuming. What do you say to the family when you destroy a thousand-dollar piece of equipment? Same thing you say when you hack their ceiling apart looking for drugs, or rip new kitchen cabinets down looking for old bullet holes. You say, "Sorry!"

Dunn looked at his watch. Forty-five minutes to kill before he visited Adele. He still had to talk to Moira's doctor at some point. Might as well do it on the way over. Guy should be home on a Sunday morning. But first he picked up the phone and dialed his sister, partly to reassure himself that she was alive.

"Hi, kid," he said when she answered. For a moment he felt tenderness toward her, as he often did during cases like these. Lots of cops come home after brutal homicides and hold their families a little more closely. Appreciating what they've got.

Rachel didn't answer for a moment. Dunn thought he could hear fuming over the line, or else it was a bad connection.

"You forgot my birthday" came her cold reply.

Dunn closed his eyes. Yes, he forgot her birthday Friday. "I've been on a case . . ."

"Saturday. I heard. She died Saturday. I was born Friday."

"You know, Rachel, I'm not so sure it was a Friday in 1965. . . . I mean, that's real cute the way you said that and all, but not entirely . . ."

"You can't even be sorry. You have to be an asshole."

Then he remembered. "Wait . . . no, I sent you a card! I didn't forget!"

He was answered with sarcasm. "Yeah, right."

"You didn't get it? I sent it . . . Let's see, I sent it *Thursday.*"

"Wow, maybe my postman died. It would have been

late, though, even if he had lived." Rachel's tone was re-
lentless.

"What is it with you, Rachel? All the rest of us were so
even-tempered and good-natured. How'd you turn out so
hotheaded? Four kids raised in the same family. You must
have been a foundling left on our doorstep."

"There's no such thing as the same family. For each kid,
the family's a different one." This was her favorite speech.
Dunn had had it easy. Her life had been hard. Dunn had
had a mother through most of it, whom Rachel could
hardly remember.

"Don't pout," he said calmly.

She began to scream. "Cut out that shitty stereotyping
of women! You always do that."

"I'm not talking about *women,* I'm talking about you."

Rachel thought this might be some further insult. She
came close to hanging up. "You are . . . attempting . . .
to put me down . . . when you . . . use words like
'pout.' I . . . don't . . . pout. I . . . have a . . . short
. . . upper lip," she explained in even, trembling tones,
bordering on hyperventilation.

So that explained twenty-six years of his sister's sulking.
"Happy birthday," he said quietly.

There was a long silence. Then she started to cry. "It's
not the birthday. It's everything else."

"Everything else," he echoed, with sensitivity, he
thought.

"I gotta go," she said. Rachel didn't like crying in front
of her brother. She hung up.

"I love you," Dunn said into the receiver.

Chapter 8

Love the One You're With

Dr. Kevin Byfield slipped the leash over the dog's head and opened his front door. As he stepped out onto his porch, the gray Crown Victoria pulled up to the curb in front of the Lowell Street bungalow. Dunn switched off a rather sloppy production of *Carmen* and got out.

"Dr. Byfield? Gabe Dunn, Salem Police. I said I'd stop over, is this a bad time?"

Dr. Byfield nudged the dog down the steps and approached the detective. "I've got to walk this dog. Can we talk on the way?"

"Sure." Dunn was grateful the doctor was willing to talk at all. Many wouldn't. "Lead on."

The doctor looked about Dunn's age—mid- to late thirties. Burgundy sweater and an Eddie Bauer jacket. Already doing well. The house was no mansion, but had seen a lot of remodeling and had a nice view of Juniper Cove, where his street dead-ended. The two men and the dog, trailing along behind like a small sheep, headed up toward Fort Avenue.

"When was the last time you saw Moira Doheny?" Dunn inquired.

"She was in earlier this week, actually. Monday, I believe. I could check for you later. Her file's at my office."

"How long was she your patient?"

The doctor thought for a moment. "Let's see—two years, maybe a bit more. Long before her accident."

Dunn glanced over his shoulder. "Nice-looking dog," he lied. "What's his . . ." he bent over. "Her name?" The overweight black Lab turned vaguely needy eyes toward him and waddled on with determination.

"I don't know. I'm baby-sitting it for a friend this week. Dog-sitting. I forgot to ask. I've been calling it Snowball. We used to have a cat, Snowball. I'm more a cat person."

Dunn looked back down. "Good name. You know, I think it's a she," he said, and smiled. "But then, you're the doctor. Can you tell me about the accident?"

"Not much to tell," he answered. "She suffered a concussion, a couple of fractures—wrist, I think. She was unconscious for several hours. We kept her in the hospital for about a week. The head injury left her with chronic, post-traumatic headaches."

"What were you giving her for them?" asked Dunn.

"Demerol. For a while, Valium, but that didn't do anything for her. I've tried various courses, I don't remember. They'd be in her file."

"What was the prognosis?"

"When was the accident? Last spring? I don't think her pain had diminished at all. I told her I knew of a few cases where after a year or two patients seemed to get better. But more commonly, if the pain lasted this long, there was a good possibility it was long term."

Dunn looked at him. "In other words, you didn't have any idea."

Dr. Byfield shrugged.

They had crossed onto Winter Island. A pheasant exploded from the brush on the opposite side of the road and streaked across their path. The two men looked back to see if the dog would react. She returned a look tinged with hope. Perhaps it was time to turn back. The pheasant had made no visual impact other than a faint, subliminal message reminding her somehow that she was hungry and out of breath.

Dunn bent down and scratched her under the chin. "Real trooper. She's a real trooper." Her eyes filled with intense gratitude. She sniffed his mouth.

"Maybe we're walking too fast for it," said the doctor, looking burdened. He sighed. "Would a dog like this really protect my home against all intruders?" They continued, strolling slowly.

"I've seen where EMT's couldn't get past a dog to save the owner's life." Dunn considered whether the owner of this dog would have that problem. He could imagine Snowball's Living Will: *Please do not take extraordinary measures to walk me after my time has come.* "On the other hand, I've gone into B and E scenes where there's a dog home and you almost have to suspect them of complicity. They just smile up at you. Had one once, the thieves bribed a Saint Bernard with a package of gourmet blueberry muffins from the victim's kitchen counter. The owner warned us before we went in that the dog could be dangerous. But when we did go in, there was the dog lying on the kitchen floor, burping quietly. The only thing left was bits of cellophane wrapper. And a shelf where the VCR had been."

The doctor nodded. "I think the other Snowball, the feline version, was more effective. At least cats can make you feel embarrassed to be there. When a cat looks at you, you feel like scum."

They reached the public landing and turned to follow the beach up toward the lighthouse. The dog was lagging more and more. Dunn nearly offered to carry her.

"Snowball, heel!" the doctor tried lamely. The dog continued waddling slowly, but a tragic expression filled her face.

"What do you know about the circumstances of the accident? Had Moira been drinking?" Dunn asked.

"Oh, let's see . . . If I recall, there was evidence of a moderate amount of alcohol, maybe some drugs. I'd have to check the file. While she was in the hospital she couldn't tell anything about how it happened. She had no memory of the accident, even where she was going or where she had come from."

"Did any of it come back to her?"

Dr. Byfield tugged on the leash. "Took her a few months. She told me eventually that she remembered being at a party. But she couldn't figure out what she was doing driving alone near the Kernwood bridge. I think she was starting to remember more and more. She asked me what she could do to get more to come back to her. Something bothered her about it. Something didn't make sense to her. I told her just give it time."

Dunn made a mental note to check the accident report. "Let me go back to the headaches for a second. What was Moira's attitude? Was she optimistic? Could she handle the pain?"

"Some of the time, yes. Some of the time, I'd have to say no. She wanted assurances that things would improve eventually. Pain's more bearable when you know it will end. But I couldn't give her any assurances."

"Did she ever talk to you about suicide?" Dunn asked.

"No, not to me. I gave her the name of a therapist I thought she should see, someone who I thought could counsel her more effectively than I could. I don't know if she looked up this woman or not."

"Could I get her name?"

"Sure. I've got her number at the house. I'll write it down for you when we get back."

Dunn asked: "Dr. Byfield, would you believe Moira was capable of suicide?"

The doctor waited a full minute before answering quietly. "Yes. I think she was capable."

Dunn looked at him in surprise.

They turned around and headed back toward the causeway. The dog seemed to recognize a return trip and perked up slightly. They didn't have to carry her. When they reached Dr. Byfield's gate, the Lab pushed ahead and led them to the door.

"How does she know this is home? Aren't you actually a stranger?" Dunn asked. He reached down to rub her neck.

Dr. Byfield laughed. "That's right. She doesn't know me from Adam. Her owner dropped her off last night and threw her bed into the middle of my kitchen floor, which, by the way, looks like some kind of leaky cedar beanbag chair. The bed, not the floor. Patched with duct tape. As long as her bed's here, and I feed her, this is home."

Dunn located a set of tags on the Lab's collar. One was shaped like a hydrant and bore testimony to the fact that she was caught up on her shots. The other was shaped like a heart and contained her name and address. "Her name's Laverne," Dunn announced.

"I don't even like dogs," Byfield said.

Dunn smiled. "Could'a fooled me."

The sound of Eugene's voice on the phone no longer did to Adele what it used to do. He was attempting to sound patient and reasonable, but to Adele he came off more like runny eggs. "Not that we have anything to worry about, Adele, but just to keep things simple, we were both at your place Friday night and Saturday morning, OK? That way the police won't hassle either of us."

"Why would I need an alibi, Eugene?"

"Why would *I* need one, Adele? Do I have to explain it

again? We don't need the cops on our backs. Let's make their job easier, OK? They'll solve her death a lot faster if we don't confuse them with any 'where were you's.' "

"What's to solve? She killed herself," Adele countered, trying to scrape off the uncooked parts of the conversation.

"Yeah. I'm just saying that if they have to do any head scratching they'll start digging in areas that have nothing to do with Moira. If she had friends with records, they become suspects even when there's no crime. You know?"

Adele was quiet. Finally she asked: "You ever going to stop, Eugene?"

"Stop what? You mean get a job?" He knew it was not a serious question. She was just trying to provoke him.

Adele shifted uncomfortably. The phone was quiet for a moment.

"You tired of gold chains around your neck? Got your nice bedroom set, your nice car, I can stop now? Thanks, Adele."

She still didn't speak, letting the dialogue congeal. It wasn't like she didn't do her part. Spent nights rolling coins and counting one's. Juggled four different bank accounts to avoid Welfare's snooping eyes, and to dilute suspicion when she brought in the rolled coins. Most of the cash didn't go into banks. She paid their bills with money orders. You keep enough in the bank to cover your rent and cover your bail. The rest you spend.

"Anyway, I got a job, remember?" Eugene added. "I'm a driver, when I can find work, which I can't at the moment. Times are tough, Adele. You sure you checked the place good? Nothing laying around that shouldn't be there?"

Adele glanced around. Nothing in her apartment was stolen. She had receipts for everything. She had never let them store merchandise here, or sledgehammers, crow-bars, scanners.

Adele had nothing to hide. "All set," she said, and hung up.

Chapter 9

Auld Lang Syne

Dunn went alone to see Adele Prada. The young woman rented a tiny worker's cottage on Upham Street, incongruously butted up against a converted Federalist mansion. The front of Adele's house was bandaged with Texture-one-eleven, and provided a nice contrast with the powdery aluminum siding on the rest of the building. No two homes on Upham shared the same architectural period. Many had been carved up or subdivided to accommodate various waves of war vets, or laborers displaced by the Great Fire downtown. Adele's house had served such a function. Her landlord had made some attempt at covering the exterior battlescars and dirt-under-the-nails with a few coats of paint. The house was doing its best to blend in.

Adele Prada opened the door wide and wore a hard, bored look. In contrast to her tough demeanor, her hallway was lined with framed prints of hands clasped in supplication and poems that began with *Dad . . .* in very large script. Adele's manner and decor seemed straight out of the Point. High crime, rusty tenements in disrepair, a heavy dependence on drugs and on framed prayers hanging on the walls. She gave the impression of a woman on her way up in the world, but not yet comfortable with up.

Adele motioned toward a chair, part of a dining-room set she seemed almost surprised to find in her dining

room. She sat across from him and lit the end of a New-
port Light, settling into a look of suspicion. A pearly ba-
nana clip caught up chemically overtreated curls into a
kind of mane. Big hair, they called it.

"What can you tell me about Moira Doheny?" Dunn
asked. Adele's face held a certain familiarity that he
couldn't place.

Her eyes narrowed. "What do you want to know?"

Warming to the attention, Adele Prada turned out to be
talkative, with a funny mixture of loquacity and caution.
She skittered around in the interview like a crab. Moira
Doheny had come onto the scene a little over two years
earlier. Adele had met her through a mutual friend.

"What mutual friend?"

Adele paused. Dunn continued: "Could it have been
'Eugene?' Or 'Chris?' Or 'J.G.?' "

Adele seemed to be considering in which direction to
dodge. She'd be a terror on the football field. Finally: "It
was Chris."

"Chris who?"

"Chris Alexei," she said with resignation. The most dangerous game you could play in this life was give a cop the
name of a partner. But in this case, this cop would know
the names. It was just the connection he was missing. "We
were at a party . . ." She started a lengthy description of
the party.

Dunn had stopped listening. *Alexei. Some sort of trouble*
. . . A bell went off. What was that kid's name? Christian
Alexei. Arrested Friday night for the Cosgroves' break-in
earlier in the week. He and Myles had picked up a guy that
afternoon trying to cash in some stolen lottery tickets at a
convenience store. Grimes. Judd Grimes. *J.G.* Another
friend of Moira's? He stared hard at Adele. Still couldn't
place the face, but the association was getting stronger.

Grimes was looking for enough cash to buy his drugs.

Sitting in the office, he was hurting sufficiently to come around in record time. *Didn't want no lockup.* He had been Alexei's wheel man for the Cosgroves' job, and undoubtedly a few others. Dunn had hoped for a connection to the Sports King theft, but Grimes seemed not to have been involved with that one. Grimes was a loser. If Alexei were any good, he probably only used him when he had to.

Judd Grimes gave the cops Chris Alexei. Dunn gave Grimes twenty-five dollars personal bail so the guy could get on with his shopping.

"Who bailed Chris out yesterday?" Dunn asked.

Adele paused. Dunn was getting tired of all the silent negotiation. He added: "Adele, I can check the bail slip. Whoever paid it will want their money back."

"Eugene," she said.

"Eugene!" *Eugene . . . s.* "Eugene in trouble, too?"

She smiled. "Not at the moment."

"Who is Eugene?"

Before she answered, he figured it out. Eugene Sollors. Adele's boyfriend. He said: "Haven't we met before?" He looked around. "Did I take this place apart once?"

She answered: "Not this place. We were living on Boston Street."

Dunn nodded, remembering. Sollors's apartment had been taken down to the studs.

"We had to move after that."

Sollors had more than a little history. He had worked occasionally with Chris. Had done some state time. According to Adele, Eugene had gone straight. He was terrified to go back in.

"Cleaned up his act. Eugene would do anything now to stay out of jail. Even got a job."

"What's his job?" Dunn asked.

"He's a truck driver. He does deliveries. It's part-time, but a job's a job."

Dunn grunted. "When did you last see Moira? Or speak with her?"

"I phoned her Friday night around ten, after Chris called from the station. I told her he'd been arrested and that I was trying to reach Eugene to make the bail."

"How did she seem?" Dunn asked.

The woman rolled her eyes. "Well, bummed. I guess the news upset her. More than I realized, huh?"

"Did she say anything? Mention any plans that night?"

"Like offing herself?" She shook her head. "No. She just thanked me for letting her know and hung up."

Dunn leaned back. "You know of anyone who might have had a reason to want Moira dead?"

Adele looked surprised. "You think she didn't kill herself?"

"You knew her well?" Dunn asked. "Do you think she could have?"

Adele fumbled. "Well, she was having bad pains . . . and then this stuff. Who else could have? Eugene was with me all night. And the next morning."

Guess that means, too, that *you* were with *him,* Dunn surmised. We've got *alibis.* Nicely done. "Anybody have a beef with her?" he asked.

She thought for a moment. Not so much remembering, as running through her options again. "Chris has a problem with Judd Grimes."

Dunn smiled. "Well, Judd did turn him in. I'd have a problem, too." The interview kept rolling back to Chris.

"No, I mean besides that," she said. "He thinks Judd was seeing Moira while he was in prison last year."

Jail was a cost of doing business for guys like Chris. Dunn recalled their lengthy interview Friday night after they picked him up. Chris could do time. Stayed out of trouble. Guys who made trouble got transferred far from home, making it hard for their people to visit. But Chris took it well, did what he was supposed to do, seized every opportunity to work off some of the stretch: good behavior, classes, AA, jobs, worked in the kitchen when he was lucky. You could shave two and a half days a month off your stretch. Some guys couldn't do time. But Chris could.

Only one problem. Every night your entire bid, you wonder who's with your woman. Makes you crazy. Wanna make yourself really crazy? You wonder if it's a cop with her.

"Was he?" asked Dunn.

Adele was holding back, sorting out a complex set of alliances, debts, and payoffs. Dunn knew the look and could hear the calculator humming. Somewhere inside she punched the subtotal key.

"If he was, he was careful," she hedged.

Come on. Give me more.

"They were seen a couple times." Grand total. "Judd's a loser. If Moira was doing anything, it was charity work. Know what I mean?"

"Did Chris know?" the detective asked.

"We never said anything to him, but I think he found out." She sighed. You do your best to protect someone . . .

Dunn had seen it hundreds of times. Inmates' visits with girlfriends began and ended with "Are you gonna wait for me?" "Will you be there when I get out?" Desperate questions with irrelevant answers. But what did they expect? Their career choice. *You pays your money and you takes your choice.*

"Chris on drugs?" asked Dunn.

"Not for the past year, not since he's been out of jail."

"So where does his money all go?"

Adele leaned back and surveyed her dining room. It was pretty clear where Eugene's money had gone. "Buys stuff. When they don't party, they shop. Chris is kind of a lone wolf. But he likes cars. Always has himself a nice car. Then he takes care of his friends. These guys do that. Eugene . . . always used to. Help out the family. Get presents for people. Makes them feel good, you know? Being generous. Chris has a grandfather he sends money to. He helped Moira's family out last year; they just never knew it was him. Then Moira started getting weird about it. He tried to buy her a dog before he went into prison. She made him take it back."

"Why?" asked Dunn.

Adele shook her head. "She was something else. A dog's worse than a ring, she told me. It was obvious he was trying to make them a family. We got a dog, we must be a family. All they needed was the white picket fence." She looked down at her own outstretched fingers. Laden with rings. None of them the right kind. "She didn't want to be his family." Adele obviously found this hard to understand. "Moira wanted too much. She really thought after a while that if Chris really loved her, he'd go straight. And he thought if she really loved him, she'd accept him for what he was. Till death do us part, he'd tell her."

Dunn thanked Adele and stood up. "Nice place. You work?" he asked, looking around on his way to the door. Ceiling fan with chandelier, wide-screen TV, a department-store painting with a little brass spotlight. Adele was buying sophistication.

"Was. Got laid off," she answered. Dunn leaned down and admired the hi-fi system. "I got receipts," she announced.

The detective smiled and left.

It was like a sick good news bad news joke: *The good news is the little woman is pregnant. The bad news is she's also dead . . .*

Dunn hadn't gotten to the good news part. He was

studying Chris Alexei from across a living room of furniture reminiscent of Moira's, like His and Her sweaters. Chris was holding on to composure like a kite in the wind. Dunn's previous experience with the dark-haired, slightly built youth had convinced him the boy was unperturbable. His only emotion had been caution. The pain now tugging at the kite string surprised Dunn.

As though any composure at all needed some explanation, Chris said: "Actually, I knew. I . . . found out last night." He rubbed the edge of his palm, then looked up at Dunn. "Can you tell me anything . . . I heard she shot herself."

"We only know that she died of a gunshot wound. Were you close to her?"

Chris looked up toward the ceiling. "Yes. You could say that. I . . . yeah, close." The pain seemed genuine. "When did it happen?" he asked.

"Sometime early yesterday morning is the best we can determine."

"While I was in jail . . ." somewhere between a question and statement.

"Chris, where did you go after you were released yesterday?" Dunn asked.

"Home. I came here. I took a shower and went to sleep."

"You were here by yourself?"

"Yeah."

"Anyone see you when you got here?"

"A friend dropped me off," Chris answered.

"Anyone after that?" asked Dunn.

"No."

"There's something else I need to ask you," Dunn said. The eyes turned back to him.

"Did you know Moira was pregnant?"

This time it was the surprise that was genuine.

"No . . ." the boy whispered. "Don't *do* this to me, man!" Chris buried his face in his fists and choked back a sob.

Dunn sat for a few minutes. Nothing more to ask right now. He felt unequipped for this part. What did the Manual say? *Well, pal, we can continue this later. I'll see myself out. Don't forget . . . court tomorrow, nine A.M.* "Do you want a glass of water?" he asked Chris. The boy didn't hear.

Dunn saw himself out.

When Dunn returned to the office around noon Sunday, Detective Daniel Braedon had scrawled the results of his phone research covering pages A through Z of Moira's address book onto the back of a Cruiser Deficiency Report form and left it on Dunn's desk. A few numbers were old or disconnected. Another few were no-answers. Two didn't know or remember the dead woman. Of the remainder, many but not all had known of Moira's pain. None knew of other reasons for despondency. Or of people who would want to hurt her. Or how she had spent her last day. The only one to talk to her that day was a Paula DeCotis, who had received a call from Moira somewhere between eleven and twelve Friday night. DeCotis lived about a block and a half from Moira. Moira had wanted to borrow her car. DeCotis couldn't accommodate her, because the car had been loaned to someone else. DeCotis had asked if Moira wanted to be contacted when the car was returned. Moira had said, in exact words according to DeCotis: "No, I have a better idea." Moira gave no indication of what she wanted the car for, only that she wouldn't need it more than a few minutes, quarter of an hour at most. End of conversation.

Dunn looked up at the map of Salem on the opposite wall. Seven minutes each way meant her target could have been almost any part of the city that time of night, and a good chunk of Peabody, Danvers, or Beverly. Her boy-friend was being held at the police station. Was she coming to bail him out? Fifteen minutes wouldn't have been enough time. Just the same, he'd check the booking form for the time of Alexei's phone call.

Unless her destination was very close by, Moira had not been intending a social call. That left a pickup or dropoff, or possibly getting word to someone who had no phone. *What was her "better idea"?*

Dunn turned the page over. The thirty-three car alleg-edly suffered a blown left headlight. No officer name, no date.

Chapter 10

Judd

Adele had come up with current addresses for Grimes and, with some persuasion, Sollors. Jake Myles began with the former and headed across the bridge to Beverly. Federal Street was about a mile up Rantoul. The detective pulled up in front of Saint Mary, Star of the Sea, which was a school by day and host to Beano games at night. Grimes's apartment house was diagonally across the street.

A man dressed in olive-green pants and an identically hued sweater was mopping the floor of the lobby Sunday afternoon when Myles pushed open the door. The detective located J. Grimes among the bank of bells. He gave it a punch. When the door finally buzzed, Myles stepped gingerly over the wet linoleum, smiling apologetically at the man in green as he passed by. The man didn't look up.

Grimes was up on the third floor. Myles opted for the stairs, stepping by a Big Wheel and a pile of cardboard boxes in the stairwell.

"Hey, partner," said the detective when the door opened. Judd Grimes screwed up his eyes trying to place the face. "How quickly they forget. Friday, you joined the team. Gave us Chris Alexei, remember?"

Grimes seemed to remember and changed his look to one of wariness. "Wha'd'ya want?" The kid looked like he had taken steroids for a few too many years.

"I want to talk about Moira Doheny," answered Myles.

"Who says I know her?"

"You saying you don't?"

By way of answer, Grimes swung the door wide and stepped back to let the policeman in. His face looked disheveled. A dirty rubber band was snarled up around the end of his tail. The rest of his hair was sadly in need of spiking.

Myles looked around the room as he sat down. Judd Grimes's life of crime had provided him a not too uncomfortable existence: VCR, color TV tuned to a Bruins game, stereo, cheap but not shabby couch, some kind of leatherette bar—currently housing a Nintendo set, an aquarium, a box of disposable cigarette lighters, and a bottle of Johnny Walker Red. Two cases of Miller beer next to the bar. The place looked like it had been assembled from other people's places.

Grimes's surroundings had a curiously temporary quality. Clearly not all his proceeds went to drugs. But his prized possessions looked like they had a short shelf life. Sort of a revolving inventory.

"How did you know her?" Myles shouted over the announcer's explanation of the melee to which the crowd was currently being treated.

Grimes turned down the TV. Might as well get this over with. No way was he going back to the station. "She's Chris's girlfriend. She just died."

"News travels fast. Then you socialize with Alexei? You didn't give us the impression the other night that you knew him that well. 'Just a job,' wasn't it? Something like that?" Myles parked one ankle over the other knee and stretched his arms out along the back of the couch. He gazed toward the aquarium giving Grimes time to get uncomfortable.

"Worked with him enough to know he had a girl,"

Grimes mumbled. He worked his tongue around in a gap where a tooth had been, or should have been.

"So what are those things?" Myles gestured toward the aquarium, grayish projectiles darting around in the milky water. The bottom was covered with bright-green sand and a grinning skull with a plastic plant sticking out one of the eye holes. Looked just like Salem Harbor.

"Mollies," the kid answered.

"Why mollies?"

"They survive. Can't kill 'em."

Despite our best efforts. "Good," said Myles. "So, what was your name doing in Moira's little book?"

"My name? It was in Moira's book? Jeez, I'm flattered. Maybe Chris gave it to her to call in an emergency."

"Great idea. You're just the guy I'd wanna call in an emergency. You ever try guppies? They last pretty good."

Grimes struggled for a moment to catch up. "Mollies is better," he said. "Don't have to feed them hardly. They eat their young. Perpetual motion, like."

Myles felt slightly sick. "Judd, when did you last see Moira?"

Grimes thought for a minute, then seemed to find some safe ground. "The night we did the Cosgroves' job. I picked Chris up at her place."

"Wednesday . . . the twenty-third? How did she seem?"

"Fine, I guess." A smile flickered across his lips. "Well, except they were having a fight."

Oh, right. They were having a fight. Yeah, that's right. A fight. First you don't know her, bud. Then you're privy to their domestic disputes. This is police work. Listen to bullshit all day. One witness after another. Question after dogged question, answers like pulling teeth, and still mostly lies. Nothing comes easy. A lot of energy, few results. Per-

petual motion it ain't. Myles looked at his watch. *At ap-*
proximately one P.M. this detective proceeded to Apartment
39, Eighteen Federal Street, Beverly, to interview Mr. Judd
Grimes who informed him that the victim had been quarrel-
ing . . . "Tell me about the fight," he said.

"He, that's Chris, brought her a gold chain. A real nice
one. She got mad at him. She said all this stuff about it
being stolen. Buncha crap! It wasn't stolen. I was with him
when he bought it. He got it at Daniel Lows." Grimes
pffffed. Grimes knew his jewelry stores.

"Women. Can't figure 'em," agreed Myles.

"He took good care of her," said Grimes, still unable to
figure 'em. "Never like hit her or nothin'. Ungrateful
bitch."

"How was he gonna take care of her from the Middleton jail?"

Grimes grinned. "I know Chris. Believe me, he woulda
been working overtime between now and his trial date to
get something set aside for her. He did last time. Bought
her a car so's she could visit him."

"How do you know all this? You do his taxes?"

Grimes denied this. He began scratching his arm.

"Oh, look," said Myles. "A new tattoo?" What he had
dismissed earlier as poison ivy now was discernibly a dag-
gerlike object with something wormlike wrapped around
it. "You're a real mess, aren't you? Try hand lotion on
that."

Upon further questioning of Mr. Grimes it was determined
that Chris Alexei was angry at the victim and expressed his
anger frequently to the witness during their commission of the
break-in at Cosgroves' Liquor on the night of January 23.
Grimes also suggested that matters were not helped when he,
Grimes, disclosed to Alexei that the victim had once made a
pass at him, which this detective finds hard to believe.

Myles paused at the fish tank on his way out. He bent down and pressed his nose against the glass. The fish went wild.

"Monsters," he mumbled.

Chapter 11

Central Street Blues

Dunn led Archie Block, the Store 24 cashier, upstairs and into the CID office. Late Sunday afternoon, the office was already getting dark. Block glanced at Billy Trinidad's desk as they passed by, expecting somehow to be signed in, processed, announced, or told to take a seat.

Trinidad was perched on the edge of his desk. Two gentlemen occupied the chairs, looking miserable. The one in the swivel chair was on the phone and sweating. The other had his head bowed, studying the floor. Dunn looked at Trinidad. "Weren't these guys in last night? You scooped them in Riley Plaza?"

"They decided to join up. We're still looking for a couple buys."

"What did they have? An ounce? How long can it take to find three ounces in this town?" Dunn asked. Trinidad's rule was three for one. Whatever we pop you with, you bring us three times that and we'll talk to the DA.

"We're not having a lot of luck apparently," Trinidad answered solemnly. "It seems there's no more drugs on the North Shore."

Dunn looked at Trinidad's guests. A couple of muffs. Unlikely they could score a cup of coffee at the double D.

"Thanks for coming down, Mr. Block," he said to his visitor. "Hank gave me the tapes from Friday night and

Saturday morning, including the ones from your shift. We think we've found where Moira Doheny comes in. We wanted you to tell us about it."

Dunn pulled a chair closer to the TV, located the tape he wanted, and shoved it into the machine. Mr. Block looked uncomfortable. A lot of establishments aimed the camera at the register, more interested in the actions of the employees than of the customers. This camera showed enough of the counter to catch faces. And one of the faces it had captured was Moira Doheny's, just after midnight, early Saturday morning. The woman appeared at the register with a white styrofoam cup and handed Block a bill, wadded up into a little ball. Black and white, no sound. Moira's features had an eerie clarity and alertness. A testimony both to the quality of the video camera and to the soundness of Dunn's theory that the woman was neither drugged nor in pain.

"Tell me everything you remember."

"That was a coffee. Regular. It's serve yourself. That's all she bought," Block narrated.

"You ever see her before?" Dunn asked.

"Oh, yes. She lives next door to the store. Comes in on my shift a lot. Trouble sleeping, she used to tell me."

"Did she talk at all that night? Say anything about headaches, or look like she was in pain? Or whether she was going to meet anybody?"

"Mmmh, no, not really. Said hi, got her coffee, and left."

"And she was alone? No one came in with her, or spoke to her in the store?"

"That's right."

The tape seemed to confirm that the encounter, at least on camera, had been brief. Moira was gone from view, and the corner of a *National Enquirer* appeared next to the register. A momentary pause while another customer was taken care of: a local witch coming in to buy a lottery ticket. Then, aside from pages flipping, no further action was forthcoming. "Oh, and the stamp," Block added, relaxed at last that the camera had not recorded him burglarizing the till during some deeply repressed impulse. Or picking his nose.

"The what?"

"She bought a stamp from the machine inside the door before she fixed her coffee," said Block. "The machine's over here," he explained, pointing six inches to the right of the TV.

"Any idea what she was mailing?"

Block shook his head. "A card, maybe? I don't remember exactly."

As Dunn walked him out, he asked: "What was she like, Mr. Block? What did you think of Moira?"

"Nice girl," the man answered.

When Dunn reentered the office after seeing Block out, Lieutenant Angeramo, chief of detectives, emerged from his inner sanctum and gestured for Dunn to join him. Angeramo's job was to bust balls. What he did beyond that was one of the greatest unsolved mysteries in the Criminal Investigation Division.

As Dunn took a seat, Angeramo closed the door and began in an unctuous tone: "Gabe. Listen. I'm not trying to put pressure on you or anything. But just tell me . . . what makes you wanna treat this as a homicide? You got every guy in the department in on callbacks. Help me try and justify all this overtime. Please."

"No way is this a suicide, Carl."

Angeramo exploded. He could only maintain the nice guy approach for the first question. Anyone who couldn't capitulate in that time frame risked acquired hearing loss in their nearest ear. After a sustained tirade of expletives and a review of every relevant department directive, Angeramo gave Dunn the signal to redeem himself.

Dunn leaned back and propped one foot on Angeramo's trash can. "OK. Here's what we got. Twenty-two-year-old girl, three months pregnant, close family, works part-time. Seems to be managing. I mean, her rent's paid. Food in the fridge."

"You found her with a suicide note typed on her machine, a gun next to her with her prints, powder burns on her hand. I've looked at your reports so far. No one you've talked to was shocked that she killed herself. What did her doctor say?"

Dunn paused. "He wasn't too surprised, either. But Moira was hanging out with some bad characters. Three thieves. One was her boyfriend. He and Moira had been arguing earlier in the week. Jake dug up a witness, and one of mine provided a motive."

"Motive for the argument or for a homicide?" Angeramo asked.

"Well, maybe both. Moira may have been fooling around while her guy was in jail. Or maybe not, but he believed she was, which is sufficient."

"Gabe . . ." Angeramo's voice was starting to rise again. "Nothing at the scene pointed to a jealous rage. It was tidy and planned."

Dunn had to agree. And Alexei had no history of violence or assault. But there were undercurrents in her relationships and in her choice of friends which bothered him. A kind of elusive volatility danced among her chums like a twister in a trailer park. Somehow, Dunn suspected Moira had unwittingly stepped in its path.

"Danny found out Moira was trying to borrow a car around midnight Friday," Dunn offered.

Angeramo snorted. "So she originally planned to drive

off the Kernwood bridge! Having failed last spring, from your reports. Look, I gotta lot of establishments pressing me on these break-ins, Gabriel. The owner of the Sports King is financially ruined. Let's get Mr. Lazarus his cards back. Help him feed his family. You're wasting a hell of a lot of resources on a case that looks pretty open and shut to me. The girl's dead. But every night some mother-fucker's hitting another store in this city."

"Yeah? Three of those motherfuckers knew Moira Do-heny," Dunn pointed out.

"Small world. You've got till Tuesday to quit blowin' smoke up my ass. Then you close this case or give me a fuckin' good reason why not."

Dunn was about to suggest his boss look at the face on the videotape. Moira's vitality seven hours before her death was reason enough. But he decided that for the moment it was more important to let Angeramo have the last word.

Myles strode in with a can of Sprite. Ignoring the muffs, he leaned toward Trinidad, who had reclaimed his seat. "I'd like to speak to a detective, honey," he said.

Trinidad gestured toward the chief's door. "They're both in there. Come back tomorrow."

"Gabe in there with Geronimo?" Myles asked. Trinidad nodded. "What's up?"

The evidence officer shrugged.

"Secret squirrel shit?" Myles whispered.

"Secret squirrel shit," Trinidad confirmed.

Myles drained the can and dunked it into Trinidad's basket. "Well, would you tell him Moira's mom's in town? I'm gonna go talk to her. That is, if he still cares. If he still has a job."

*   *   *

The phone was ringing before Dunn reached his desk. Trinidad answered it, then put it on hold. It was Warren Carlson, Dunn's brother-in-law.

"Want to go for a run?" Warren asked when Dunn picked up.

Dunn paused, looked at his watch, out the window, and at the pile of messages on his blotter. "Sure, why not. Just make it short and slow." He hadn't run in weeks.

After Trinidad filled him in on Myles, the detective changed into shorts and caught up with Warren in front of Pickering Wharf. The two headed down toward the Willows. New Derby Street was ravaged with road work, unusual for this time of year. Ice, cars, and barricades made the first few blocks unsociable. Finally they left downtown behind and found a comfortable pace side by side.

"What's up with my sister?" asked Dunn.

"Rachel?" Warren responded. "I don't know. Tired, I think. January's a rough time to have kids."

"Oh, February's better?" asked Dunn.

"Shorter. February's shorter. I've been telling her to take it easy. She has an uncanny ability to draw crises into our lives when we're momentarily experiencing accidental tranquility." Warren was an English teacher at Salem High. "I think she needs a vacation, or a trip to the doctor, or both."

"You think anything's wrong with her?" asked Dunn, who had assumed, despite her protestations, that the birthday was the problem.

"Nothing she's shared with me," Warren answered. "How's your suicide coming?"

"I'm not sure it was a suicide, Warren."

"Why?"

"I don't think she had strong enough reason to die. But no one agrees with me. She had a lot of pain and not much hope."

"Untreatable pain?"

"So far. But her doctor didn't impress me a whole lot. Why didn't this woman get other opinions? Go to a couple of specialists? She just let it blow her off course. Maybe she did have a problem with hope."

They were abreast of the power plant on Fort Avenue. The plant was gatekeeper to the Willows, and the reputed source of all problems in the neighborhood since it appeared forty years ago. Despite it being a gentle and sensitive neighbor by everyone's admission, for four decades the local refrain had been "Blame it on the power plant!" to everything from ash on the cars to burnt dinners. Kids in the Willows grow up crazy. People blame it on the plant.

Dunn was keenly aware that Warren was holding back his own pace. The detective was more used to short, fast sprints ending up in dumpsters. His knee was bothering him, and his pride. It was certainly reassuring that the city's teachers were in better shape than its police department.

"Even in the absence of hope, our instinct to survive remains. For many people that's all they have. Don't underestimate it. Remember Sisyphus?" asked Warren.

"Remember what?"

"In Homer."

"You're the English teacher. I'm just a cop," said Dunn.

"Ever read Camus?"

"I'm just a cop," repeated the cop.

They had passed the ball field at the entrance to the park and headed down along the arcade. At the end of the park was a beach and pier, their destination.

"Sisyphus was the one the gods punished by making him roll a giant boulder to the top of a mountain. Over and over again. Whenever he got to the top, it would roll back down again. It was supposed to be the worst punishment imaginable. Worse than having birds peck at your liver, or turning to stone. The worst punishment in life is struggling without hope. Toiling in futility. But Sisyphus never gave up."

"Look—problems at home, I can deal with. Problems with the gods, not my territory."

"The essential question, as Camus says, the only serious question in philosophy, is whether life is worth living," Warren continued.

Dunn said nothing. Down by the popcorn stand a band of gulls up to no good scattered as they passed. Winter stand-ins for the Hell's Angels. The detective had no answer to Camus's essential question.

"In the face of such punishment, what kept him going?" asked the English teacher, as if expecting his brother-in-law to solve this nearly three-thousand-year-old mystery.

"What was Camus's answer?" asked Dunn, mostly out of politeness.

Warren laughed. "He believed Sisyphus was happy. And he got himself a Nobel prize."

"Sisyphus?" asked Dunn, bewildered.

"No, Gabriel." Warren gave up on the conversation. Saved his patience for tenth-graders. They needed every bit of it.

"I wonder what Moira was being punished for?" mused Dunn. They turned at the pier and headed back to town.

Chapter 12

Iris

Moira Doheny's mother, Iris, had just arrived from LA and was staying Sunday night at Sasha's. Jake Myles went by to talk to her. He had put on a fresh shirt with parrots and palm trees, hoping she'd feel more at home.

Iris Perlmutter now, the woman explained she had divorced Clarence nearly five years ago and went out to California a year later. She had a brother out there, and young nieces and nephews. A bar owner named Steven Perlmutter had convinced her to stay.

For the trip Iris had worn a navy-blue running suit with fire-engine-red lipstick and sneakers with some actress's trademark. Her hair was a nonoriginal shade of brown. Her eyes, struggling to deny her age, were ringed with streaked eyeliner.

"Mrs. Perlmutter, were you close to your daughter?"

"Yes. We were very close." She spoke quietly. Someone had given her a tranquilizer. Myles could see the flight had taken its toll. "We talked almost every week on the phone."

"When did you last hear from her?" he asked.

"We were very, very close," she repeated.

"When, uh, did you last talk to her?" Myles tried again. She looked at Myles as if seeing him for the first time.

"Wednesday or Thursday, I'm not sure which," she answered at last.

"Did she seem more depressed than usual?"

"She was feeling lonely, I remember. And bothered by things. I suppose she was sort of depressed," Mrs. Perlmutter said.

"What was bothering her?"

The woman didn't respond. She seemed to be drifting a bit.

"Mrs. Perlmutter? Did she tell you she was pregnant? Was that on her mind?" Family could be so difficult.

"I . . . yes, I knew she was pregnant. I don't think she told anyone else. Not even Sasha. My other daughter."

"Why not?" Myles asked.

"Moira wasn't sure what she was going to do about it. She'd been taking so many painkillers. Some not even approved by her doctor. I don't know how she got ahold of some of them."

"She had friends, Mrs. Perlmutter, who could get her anything she wanted."

"Oh. Chris? He was a problem, wasn't he," she said.

"Yes, ma'am. He was a problem." Myles shifted in his chair.

"She thought the baby would be affected by some of the medications. And she wasn't sure what kind of life she'd have with someone like Chris . . . not a good father figure for a child."

"She was planning to stay with Chris?"

Mrs. Perlmutter looked puzzled. "Actually I'm not sure. I think she was trying to . . . to outgrow him. To work through him."

Talked California already. "How did she get mixed up with guys like that?" Myles asked her.

"I don't remember how the two met. Chris was always rather sweet. Quiet, but sweet. I had a feeling she was experimenting with being, well, *wild* for a time. Chris was an opportunity, but a pretty safe one."

"Safe?" Myles either didn't speak California or didn't speak Woman.

"She knew he would never hurt her. And I think he stopped using drugs when he met her. That's what she told me," said Moira's mother.

We always tell our mothers that. Myles pulled out his notebook and a pen. *M. considering abortion.* He scratched his head. "So, Mrs. Perlmutter, would you say Moira was considering an abortion?"

"She didn't like the idea of an abortion. That was why she was troubled, I think." Mrs. Perlmutter looked around the room. She hadn't been back East in a long time and she wondered how Sasha had been doing. Not many pictures on the walls. No photographs at all. She looked back at Myles for help in finding her place. Myles was scratching out something in his notebook. "Where were we?" she asked.

"I was wondering myself . . ." he began.

"You know, when you're young and alone, you can pretend all you want. Pretend to be daring, take risks, cut loose, just try on that sort of life for a while. But then when suddenly you become a parent, all that changes. You still fight with wanting to stay young, but now there's a sort of clean slate. A new chance. And a responsibility. And you think, 'I'm not going to make all those mistakes my parents made. Or all those other grown-ups. I'm still young and . . . *wise*. The way only the young can be. *I'm* going to be the *perfect* parent!' Do you know what I'm talking about?" she asked. Her eyes were shining.

"No." Myles answered. That's some tranquilizer, he thought. He wrote in his notebook: *M. keeping baby— dumping C.A.* "So, you're saying she was going to keep the baby?"

She looked slightly taken aback. "Did I say that?"

Gimme a break, woman!

Mrs. Perlmutter went back to looking for family photographs on Sasha's inhospitable walls. "Boys are harder, Officer," she said in a pained voice. "You know, they push us away sooner, but they need us so much longer."

"Can I take it Moira had a brother?" Myles asked, but got no answer. He wished Sasha would come home. Put the mother out of her misery. Maybe shooting her would do it. He'd do it for her. Had the Smith & Wesson right here. Thirteen rounds.

"Mrs. Perlmutter, did she ever talk to you about suicide?"

She looked at him. "You know, there were moments when she was ecstatic thinking about the baby. She'd allow herself that. Let it slip through for a few moments. But then her mood would swing back. Back to worrying. Parenthood. Not an easy thing."

Myles studied a mole in the middle of the woman's forehead. *Right there. Could plug her right there.* "Was she suicidal? Did she talk about killing herself?" he asked, with tension in his jaw.

"Have you any idea what it's like for a parent to watch their child go through that for the first time? Their own personal discovery of parenthood? It's so delightful . . . They think they're inventing the experience."

"No, ma'am." Myles bent down over his notebook. *Fruitcake,* he wrote. He drew two lines under the word. "Did she ever tell you she planned on killing herself?"

She stared at him. "Never. She never would have entertained the thought. Even in her worst moments of pain. She would cry into the phone, Officer, she'd say, 'Momma, make it *stop!*' I couldn't do anything for her." Mrs. Perlmutter started to cry. "Couldn't do anything."

Myles looked down at his parrots and palm trees. He

didn't know what more he could do for this woman. "Mrs. Perlmutter, other family members didn't seem surprised at the suggestion that she took her own . . ."

"Other family members weren't her *mother!*" she shouted.

Myles drew a few more lines under the previous ones and shut his notebook. *Beam me up, Scotty.* "Yes, ma'am."

Out in the car he threw the notebook on the seat beside him. Now he had to go write the fucking report.

Sasha had insisted on grocery shopping by herself. She had somehow convinced her mother that a long trip required rest and had even managed to switch the effect of the time zones. Doped up on Valium, Iris had agreed to stay at the house. Sasha had always thought of her mother as Iris. Moira had called her Mom.

Not particularly anxious to get back, Sasha was doing the whole store. Every aisle, shopping by process of elimination rather than from a list. Apparently her pace just matched that of a deaf couple going in the opposite direction. The two carts passed each other at the same spot in the middle of each aisle. For the first two times, she had been amused. For the next two encounters, she began to worry that they would think she was spying on them. Maybe she was following them to watch them do funny things with their hands. In aisle five, however, the woman smiled at her, forgiving her.

Sasha was standing in the International section. Foods from around the world. She was struck with inspiration and reached for a box of Enchilada Dinner. That and her package of Cape Cod potato chips should make a nice welcoming meal for her mother. A little blend of East and West. Sasha considered her relationship with Iris. Somehow the mother-daughter thing that Moira had experienced had always eluded Sasha.

* * *

Dunn and Myles were waiting for their suppers. So were the usual Sunday-night flock of Salem State College students, bouncing into the sub shop like sailors on leave.

"What'd you get from the mother?" Dunn asked.

"She's a tune," answered Myles.

"Well, she *is* from LA."

"Moira was 'working through' Chris," Myles elaborated.

"To get her head in a better place?"

"Her head and other parts of her body, I guess."

"Well, you do what you have to do," said Dunn.

Their orders were announced. Myles grabbed a couple of cans of Coke from the refrigerator and met Dunn back at the booth. They shared the bench facing the front door; no cop sits with his back to an entrance. Dunn propped the radio next to the napkin holder and unwrapped a meatball sub the size of his leg.

The guys in the department referred to Luigi's Submarine Sandwiches as the substation. Down on Lafayette, it was the traditional location where informants could drift in and talk to cops. You have information, you need information, you drop by the substation. Dunn wasn't expecting anything today, other than supper.

"So she was unable to shed any light on who exactly Moira is?" Dunn asked. His biggest problem with this case was the victim. How'd she end up with this crowd? If he could just understand her a little, he'd have half a chance in figuring out why she was now dead.

Myles shook his head. "After meeting Mom, I'm surprised Moira didn't take a few hostages down with her."

Dunn looked at him without listening. "What do we know about her, Jake?"

Myles swallowed some Coke. "She was into garbage regeneration. Grew carrots from carrots." He bit into his veal cutlet sandwich.

Dunn decided to drop it.

"What about you? Anything?" Myles continued with his mouth full.

"I think I want to look into her old car accident. The little she remembered apparently bothered her. If it bothered her, it should bother us," Dunn said.

"OK. We're bothered. Anything else?"

"I'm still trying to chase down this guy Sollors. His girlfriend doesn't know where he is today. Actually, we know him. His picture's up in the office and he's in our computer."

"Which computer?"

"He's in everyone's computer. We've got Sollors, Grimes, Alexei—they're all in each other's 'known associates' files. Board of Probation query went through a box of paper when we mentioned their names." Dunn sipped his Coke. "Didn't they have any milk?" he asked.

"Real men don't drink milk. Have a clue, Gabe."

"Anyway," Dunn continued, "Judd Grimes is a nothing. Sollors and Alexei are career guys. Sollors has got twice the history Alexei has, but I think it's because Alexei is twice as smart. He's never been caught during a B and E. But the way he pulls them off, you know he's a professional. Lots and lots of practice."

"How does he get caught then?"

"Twice he's been ratted out by his buddies. Earlier he was sloppy. Possession of class-A substance, possession of burglarious tools, operating unders, a couple of burglaries before he got the hang of it. Chris Alexei could clear hundreds of cases for me if we could just be friends."

"Talk to him. Just like you're talking to me. He'll understand, I know he will."

Chapter 13

The Gatekeeper

Later Sunday evening, the witness to Moira's accident, Selma Fecteau, parted one of several layers of lemon-yellow window dressings and gestured out toward the Kernwood Golf Course across the street from her bungalow. "Just over there. I heard the crash. When I looked out it was flipped over in the Cold Springs ravine. I called 911. They connected me to the police."

Moira's license history had netted Dunn the date and location of her accident. Sargent Street and Kernwood Avenue, Salem, April 29. In the Traffic Department downstairs, he dug up a copy of the accident and journal reports. The original caller now sat wheelchair-bound before him trying to recollect the night. She had never seen the vehicle before, could remember no unusual sounds prior to the crash. No one walking by that she recalled. But then it had been dark. Between the pools of light provided by the street lamps, armies could have been encamped without her notice. But the police department had only one recorded call.

"Of course, I couldn't do anything myself to help. I deeply regret that," she said with disappointment.

"But you did help," Dunn told her. "No one could have done more until rescue arrived. And no one else called in. You saved that young woman's life. She was lucky—you're the only house around."

She nodded and accepted his reassurance with gratitude. "So she recovered? The papers never said."

"Yes, she did."

She smiled. "That's good." Mrs. Fecteau surveyed the room for him. "This is actually a gatekeeper's cottage, you know. It's very quiet all around here. Cemeteries, woods, the golf course, no other living persons until Cabot Farm, down toward Kernwood Bridge."

Dunn nodded politely, disappointed that this gatekeeper held no key.

Mrs. Fecteau looked back at Dunn. Concern revisited her face. "And the other one?" she asked.

"Other one what?" asked Dunn, not understanding.

"The young boy. The driver. Was he all right?"

Dunn stared at her. "Driver?" Nothing in any of the reports mentioned a second occupant. Moira Doheny had been thrown clear of the car, and had been presumed to be driving.

"He looked like he was in better condition. He was scrambling out when I looked out. I thought, in fact, that he was going to look for a phone. Didn't they talk to him?"

"You didn't mention this when you called in?"

"I thought I did, I'm not sure. I think the policeman who took the call just asked if anyone was hurt."

"Can you describe him at all?"

"No, not really, just looked like a young man in the dark."

"And where was he headed?"

"Up to the road . . . well, the bushy area next to the road. I didn't see him after that, when I came back from the phone call. You know, maybe he slipped out of my mind when I was talking to the police."

Just slipped out. Stole away into the night.

*　*　*

Lynn, Lynn, city of sin

James Deemer had been brought in by one of the beat officers for shoplifting steaks from a supermarket on Highland Avenue. Personal bail was set at twenty dollars. Deemer couldn't make it.

It was just after eight P.M. Myles was typing up some of the day's results while Dunn went to Kernwood Avenue. The January winds blew through the cracks around his window with gale force, reaching him past the stretches of duct tape and beyond the protective barricade of manuals on the sill, placed there to stop the snow from drifting in. Deemer was brought up so that Myles, in his official capacity of department photo and print man, could take a Polaroid snapshot of him against the back of the office door. According to the tape measure glued to the doorjamb, Deemer stood five feet six inches. Slightly built, dirty-blond hair in a scruffy ponytail, and tracks up and down both arms. The guy was from Lynn. He didn't seem to recall how he had gotten to Highland Avenue. Once he was processed, Myles returned to his typewriter. Deemer was taken back downstairs, put into Cell two and given a blanket. His jacket, belt, and shoes were thrown into a yellow laundry basket out in the hall with a number two painted on the bottom.

A significant portion of police work in solving a case consists of calling the snitches, and making deals in the booking room. And waiting for tips. The tips one doesn't anticipate, or think to go after. A detective is heavily networked, or he's ineffectual. A distant bell sounded in Myles's head. He flipped off the typewriter again and turned to paw through the papers on his desk. The query on Judd Grimes surfaced. Previous address: 22 Semple Street, Lynn, Massachusetts. Last assault charge was in Lynn, in October.

Myles stood up and put on his jacket. It was twenty-eight degrees outside. The lockup would probably be twenty-nine. He headed downstairs to try to convince James Deemer to join the team. On the way he stopped at the front desk and grabbed the printout on him. One entry. A prior shoplifting arrest about a month earlier. No wants or warrants.

The detective frowned. This scant biography hardly fit his friend in Cell two. The guy shook whenever he stood up. The printout could not possibly be his entire life's story. Myles had them query the computer again, running the license number, and every variation and cross-reference they could think of. Nothing.

Myles went into the lockup, leaned against the bars, and rapped on the plexiglass. Deemer stirred somewhere under his gray blanket. Only the top of his head was visible. "I'd like to talk to you, James."

"What do you want?" was the muffled reply.

"Ever hear of a guy by the name of Judd Grimes?"

"Who?"

"Big kid. Muscular. Blond, short hair with a tail. Missing a front tooth. Ring any bells? Had some trouble down in Lynn recently."

"Don't know him" from deep within the blanket. The man was still shaking. Myles wondered if he would have known his own mother.

"Talk to *me*," said a voice from the bunk in Cell three. "I know people."

Myles ignored the interruption. "So what's your real name, James?"

"I told you. James Deemer."

"He told you. Name's Beamer." Again the solo Greek chorus from the next cell.

"C'mon, James. Don't jerk me around," Myles said.

" 'Buzzard's luck, cop . . .' " Cell three wouldn't shut up.

"I swear. It's my name."

" 'Can't kill nothin' . . .' " said his neighbor.

Myles stepped back. "We'll see." He could see the condensation from his breath. He put up the collar of his jacket.

" '. . . and nothin' will die.' "

Myles went upstairs.

The files were kept in the office next door to CID. The detective let himself in and pulled the original report on the prior arrest. At the time another man had been arrested with Deemer. Further digging netted him a couple of phone numbers, and Myles reached for the phone.

"What can you tell me about James Deemer?" he asked Deemer's friend after a few preliminaries.

"I want my car, man." The price for the information. Up front.

"What's with your car?" Myles asked.

The car was at Chico's Tow, where it had been since his arrest. A 1988 Cadillac. But Deemer's friend didn't have the cash to get it back at the time. And with each passing day the amount went up twenty dollars.

"We'll take care of it," Myles said. "Who's James Deemer?"

Dmitriopolous. James Dmitriopolous. Myles called down for an NCIC query and was rewarded with four feet of history. Board of Probation provided another six. *Rumplestiltskin.* Fifteen aliases, five social security numbers. Six dates of birth. Warrants outstanding in Florida and New Hampshire. The detective called the Fort Lauderdale Police Department and relayed the good news. They asked for a fax of his prints. He couldn't raise anyone in New Hampshire other than the answering machine. He left a message and went down to the cells.

"Well, we found out who you are," Myles said triumphantly as he turned the key in the door to Cell two.

The blanket barely stirred. "Who am I?"

Myles rattled off a few of the names. "They'd like to see you in New Hampshire and they'd like to see you in Fort Lauderdale. And Worcester, but that's just little stuff. You can forget Worcester. I think you're going to Florida. They're willing to extradite."

"I don't know what you're talking about. I never heard of those names. I'm cold. Can I get another blanket?" He sat up and felt for the floor with his feet.

"Hey, I'm cold, too," said the voice from Cell three. Cell one was empty. A paper sign was taped to the bars warning that the toilet was broken.

Myles swung open the door. Deemer looked up. "What do you want now?" he whined.

"Come on out. I have to fingerprint you."

Deemer rubbed his head. "So where am I now?" His words were slurred.

"Ain't Kansas anymore," answered Cell three.

Myles led Deemer out into the hall and took two sets of prints. Deemer asked about the warrants and about where Myles got all the misinformation.

Myles handed him a paper towel and a pencil. "Sign here, on the back. Both cards."

The man tried to focus his eyes on the end of the pencil. After a pause he asked: "Which name should I use?"

"Use your real one. Hey, use whatever fucking name you want."

The man scribbled George Bush on each card.

As the detective locked him back up, Deemer said: "Can I make my call? When do I get to make my call?"

"I'll send someone down," Myles said.

"I wanna make my call, too," yelled the voice from the next cell.

Deemer was fully awake now. "Hey, can I pick where I go? Can I go to New Hampshire? Like tonight?"

"Get in some skiing," recommended Cell three.

"You have to be arraigned first. Then they can all come and get you. Tomorrow. If you don't want to go to Florida, you can elect to fight that one. But in the end, it's not your choice. It's probably gonna be whoever's got the bigger beef."

Deemer looked glum. "Can I make my call now?"

The voice from Cell three yelled, "Florida. Go to Florida."

Myles got the blanket and slid it through the narrow gap below the plexiglass. The detective thrust his hands into his pockets and shivered. "Yeah, I'd pick Florida."

He turned and went back upstairs.

Chapter 14

We Got Tonight

Back at his desk, Dunn picked up the phone and dialed Sasha Doheny. It was after ten Sunday night. When she answered, he asked if she had any knowledge of who the driver might have been the night of the accident. Sasha had always thought that Moira had been alone. Dunn described his talk with Mrs. Fecteau.

"Are you sure?" she asked. Then: "You know, Moira never did regain full memory of that night. It was always puzzling her. Dr. Byfield said she might never remember. Or that it might suddenly come back to her someday."

"What did she remember? Anything?"

"She told me she was at Adele's. They were just hanging out there, a party of some kind. Then when she left . . . she didn't remember much after that. She said it was dark on Kernwood Avenue and she thought she might have seen an animal, a cat or something. She wasn't sure. And she didn't remember what she did, whether she swerved or braked or what. Woke up in the hospital."

"Maybe she doesn't remember swerving or braking because she wasn't the one driving. And she was on Sargent Street, according to our accident reconstructionist. That's a dangerous road at night. Lots of people take the wrong turn at the cemetery, think they're on Kernwood, but they end up on Sargent. They blow the stop sign at the end 'cause Kernwood doesn't have one. Just when they think they've reached the bridge, they're over the embankment. Sasha, if you think of anyone who might have been with her, or who might know, call me," he said.

Dunn tried Adele next. Her line was busy, so he went down his list of names. There was' no answer at Chris Alexei's or Eugene Sollors's. He reached Judd Grimes, who barely remembered Moira's accident, much less who her companion might have been. Finally, Adele's line was clear.

Adele hung up. The detective, Sergeant What's-his-face, had just told her Moira had not been alone in the car at the time of the accident. The news shocked her. She had assumed until now that Moira left the party by herself that night.

Eugene was stretched out on the couch watching a Chuck Norris movie. "Eugene," she asked, hand still on the receiver, "do you remember anyone being with Moira that time she ran off the road?"

"What time? That party here? I don't even remember her leaving." His eyes were fixed to the TV.

Adele went into the bathroom to resume brushing her teeth. Friends stopped by lots of nights. She had a hard time bringing to mind that particular night. It probably constituted a party because the music was cranked up and more than a half dozen people were around. Plenty of booze and drugs. She thought harder, trying to reconstruct the events surrounding the accident. Well, except that night they did run low. A lot had been consumed. Moira had consumed her share. What was it they were low on . . . just beer? Someone . . . who was it? . . . had volunteered for a packie run, but there was some problem. What was the problem? She strained to recall. Adele spat into the sink.

* * *

Alone in the detectives' office, Dunn attempted unsuccessfully to ward off his frustration and fatigue. He had filled Myles in and sent him home. The interesting turn had so far been a dead end. He stood up heavily, flipped on the answering machine, pulled on his jacket, shut out the lights. *We're losing the beat.*

Dunn descended the back stairs in pitch dark. Somehow the department never managed to keep a working bulb in the back stairwell. Waste of money. The public wasn't supposed to use this staircase and members of the force knew the way in their sleep. Marble stairs continued on down where logic would have placed a landing. Someday they were going to get their asses sued.

The back door led out to the front of the building same as the front door, depositing its users by the cars on Central Street. Feeling weary and irritable, Dunn decided to take the gray car home for the night. As he opened the door he noticed twenty-seven car, one of the cover cars, had pulled in. He could just make out Officer Paul Szymanski by the dim light of the streetlight, sitting in the cruiser and holding something to his face. Dunn walked over. He leaned in the window and asked: "What's up, bud?"

Szymanski pulled the rag away and examined a smear of blood. "I caught a domestic. Violent domestic, in a car, down on Webb Street."

Dunn nodded sympathetically. "You OK?" Disputes, especially domestics, were some of the most dangerous calls a cop could answer. Talk about No Win.

Szymanski snorted. "I pull up on them, you know, blew down there with lights and siren, aimed the fucking takedown lights in their faces. Never noticed me. Wailing away at each other in the front seat, elbows jabbing at the horn, fur flying. So I yank open the door and haul them out.

She's screamin' at me *arrest that sonofabitch* and I'm trying to separate them. She's sayin' she's gonna leave him, he's sayin' he's gonna kill her, you know, usual stuff. So I says, 'You're coming with me, buddy.' So then he leans toward her and hollers, *'Now* look. See what I'm gonna hafta do? I'm gonna hafta beat this cop!' "

Dunn laughed. "And then he did?"

Szymanski grimaced painfully. "They both jumped on me. She's on my back, he's hammering at me while I'm messing with the cuffs. Finally got him jacked up against the side of the car, bitch's still hangin' on my neck. Got him cuffed, got her cuffed, *then* my backup rolls in."

Dunn shook his head in disbelief. "Well, if anyone could've done it, you could, lapper. Where are they now? Inside?"

Szymanski nodded. "Gave them each a room. Room with a view." The affectionate term for the lockup.

Dunn turned to go. "Get someone to look at that lip, pal."

Are we heroes, or what.

When Dunn got home it was nearly midnight. Flyers from yesterday, soggy with snow, still littered his doorstep. No food in the house, too late to call his sister for a free meal, even if she were on speaking terms with him. He felt his depression growing steadily into despondency. Szymanski's lip bothered him. The whole fucking job bothered him.

His original plans for the evening got shit-canned with the murder. Dinner with a lady, possibly celebrating his soloing this weekend, possibly some other excuse. His plans with Mel Isaksen had gone astray more often than not.

Dunn wanted to call her, because even though it was late and she would be asleep, he knew it would be all right.

It would be OK, but it wouldn't be fair to her. Dunn wasn't really thinking about Mel or their new and tentative relationship. He was thinking about Claire, his ex-wife. Mel deserved to be thought about. Claire did not. But his relationship with Mel was not mysterious. Uncertain, yes. But understandable. With Claire, he had been certain. His current nonrelationship with her was the biggest mystery of his life.

Claire had left nearly five years earlier, taking their daughter, Joy. She had gone home to a small, grungy town in New York, repudiating her life so completely that she had refused to stay in New England, much less in North Salem with Dunn. Gabe Dunn had turned thirty-seven last November. Next fall he had hoped to walk with his daughter when she marched off, lunchbox in hand, to her first day of school. To help her find her room and find her way.

Now he didn't even know his own way. After five years he still didn't understand.

Dunn dropped the wet flyers into the trash. He had one phone message. He stabbed at the button and poured himself a glass of orange juice.

"Gabe? It's Mel, just checking to be sure you're OK. Call if you feel like it. Doesn't matter how late. Bye, bye."

It would be so easy. Easy to lose himself in her. He stared down into the glass. A Celtics glass he got at a Mobil station.

All day long on the job the people love you, hate you, depend on you, hold you accountable, crush you, need you, and you respond to it all. What's left when you go home? You've given everything you have.

What was he going to give Mel?

Dunn didn't see enough happy families to believe in them anymore.

*   *   *

Adele sat on the edge of her bed and let the quiet enfold her. Eugene had gone out. Chuck Norris had shut up. In the five years she had known Eugene, they had rarely slept the night together. Adele had no intention of changing to his schedule. To Adele, nights were for sleeping. Days were for shopping. Their only quality time was mornings. Mornings were for sex. She lay back and stared toward the ceiling she couldn't see.

It was a Sunday night, that night. That was the problem. Liquor stores were closed in Massachusetts. Judd Grimes had a case at home, so he told Adele he'd get it. Adele had lost track after that. And then Moira had just disappeared at some point with no announcement. It wasn't with Chris, he was still in jail. He got out the following month just after Moira was released from the hospital. Eugene . . . it wasn't Eugene. He was around all night. Life of the party. She remembered now: Eugene and Judd had argued because Judd had wanted to borrow Eugene's car for the run and Eugene said no. Judd's own wheels were in Lynn somewhere, probably impounded or seized . . . *But then Judd was gone. And the case of beer never showed up . . .*

At one A.M. he still couldn't fall asleep. Dunn felt for the phone by his bed. He dialed Mel's number and waited a long time until she answered. He couldn't give, but he could still take.

"Can I come over?" he said.

Chapter 15

Just the Two of Us

At four in the morning, TV fare has its limitations. But to a man who works nights, this is prime time. Eugene Sollors had flipped back and forth between *PT 109* and auto racing for the past half-hour. He finished off the last of a package of Pinwheels and chased them down with a can of Jolt.

Sollors looked at his watch. What he needed was an all-night gym. He felt like working out. Followed by a sauna and session in the tanning booth. He picked at the skin on his wrist. Starting to fade already. He hated pale, white skin. Made him feel like he'd just gotten out of prison. Fish-belly skin.

He channel-surfed. *Show Boat* was playing on the Disney channel. He knew this stuff from somewhere. Pretty lame. But Sollors put down the remote control, opened another can of Jolt, and in a few minutes started to sing. *Getta little drunk, and ya lan's in jaaaaaay . . . uhl.* This was cool.

Adele had learned to sleep with foam ear plugs and a sleep mask on nights Eugene was around. It wasn't always enough. She got up and closed the bedroom door more tightly. She got up again and pushed a small throw rug against the crack at the bottom of the door.

The colors on the screen were heavy on the oranges. No

blues or greens in those days, he guessed. *I git's weary and sick of tryin'* . . . Sollors searched around for some self-pity. *I'm tired of livin'* . . . he bellowed out with feeling, two and a half steps higher than William Warfield.

Adele turned on the radio by her ear. She cranked up WSSH and suffered through a selection of that travesty known as "soft rock." Music hazardous for diabetics. If rock charged your soul, soft rock embalmed it. Pinned you to your bed, or the elevator, or aisle four, or whatever.

Finally an Anne Murray cut convinced her to give up. Adele swung her feet to the floor, folded a sweater around her shoulders, and staggered out into the living room. There was Eugene, can of soda held high over his head, trying to cry. . . . *and scared of dyin'* . . .

"Where'd you go tonight?" she tried to yell over the music.

"What?" Sollors yelled back. *But ol' man river, he jes' keeps rollin'* . . .

"WHAT DID YOU HIT?" she screamed.

. . . *aaah . . . looooong!* Finally he looked at her. "Bar."

"I love the kids, I hate the system." Mel sat up and pulled on a pair of red-and-white tube socks she had fished from the floor. It was five-thirty A.M. on a school day.

Dunn handed her a cup of coffee and sat down beside her with his own. "You're burned out." A little of the tentativeness in their relationship had drained away.

"I hate that word. I never thought I'd join the ranks of burned-out teachers. I thought, there are exceptions. They must be the truly dedicated . . ."

"Or the truly crazy. There's no shame in burnout. It's a healthy response. Staying is what's not healthy." He began rubbing the back of her neck.

"There's so much I could do, Gabe. But they've cut out

so much, so many services, there's days when I have just one aide and six kids, seven this year. We spend the whole school day feeding and toiletting them, fighting broken wheelchairs, struggling with leg braces they've outgrown . . ."

"Stop it."

". . . and what's down the road? What do they graduate to? Adult programs have been cut, group living's cut back, more and more get shuffled to Fernald to sit parked in a hallway all day. So I suppose I shouldn't care that I don't have time to teach them how to feed themselves now. When they're twenty-two no one will have time to let them."

"Mel. Quit." He stopped rubbing and encircled her neck with his hands.

"They'll just pour thin gruel down their throats," she said.

"And you complain about *my* job. Yours is far more disgusting. Your morning snack time is worse than anything I've seen on the street. Give me a six-car pile-up on Route 114 anytime."

She looked appalled. "You're a wimp. I didn't know this about you."

"Mel, we have the same problem. I catch the same bad guy every week for six years. Same charge, same disposition. Good cases each time, but I still see him out on Lafayette a week later. You see kids year after year and their objectives don't change. 'Cause they never progress. How many years can you teach a kid to tie his own shoe before you lose heart?"

"Some learn," she said sadly.

"And then summer programs get cut, what happens?" he reminded her.

"We start over in the fall. And at Fernald they get shoes without laces."

He released the stranglehold and cradled her face in his hands. "What do you want to do with your life, Mel?"

"I thought maybe welding. I could go into welding. What about you?"

He smiled sadly. "I dunno. I'm only trained to push boulders up hills."

Chapter 16

Will You Still Love Me

Monday Myles was in early. The woman on the desk said George Bush wanted a word with him. He wasn't due to be taken to the courthouse for over an hour. The prisoner was hungry and had some information. Myles went into the lockup.

James Dmitriopolous, aka Deemer, was sitting up wrapped tightly in his blankets. His bare feet hung motionless, gray as steel, except for yellowed toenails. His eyes looked a bit clearer. His skin still looked like it could use a good coat of sealer. "Who was that dude again?" he asked as soon as Myles approached.

The detective answered, "Judd Grimes." It hardly mattered. Hungry inmates knew everyone. And the smell of a courthouse deal sorely whetted the appetite.

"Oh, yeah. Know him."

Myles smiled.

"Guy's big. One tooth gone," Deemer said to establish his credentials.

Sonofabitch was actually listening last night, thought Myles. "Yeah, just like I told you. Now tell me something I don't know, James."

"That the guy who's always grabbing lighters?"

Grimes had indeed cleaned Cosgroves' out of Bic disposable lighters. The police had found four in his pockets when they arrested him.

Myles leaned closer. "You saying he's an arsonist?"

Deemer shook his head. "Nah, just gives 'em to people. Said he'd give me some. But I don' smoke. You know, pollutes the body."

"James, your mom would be proud. Anything else? Other than kleptomania?"

Deemer was still considering the pollutants in his body. He finally looked up at Myles. "Can I get some breakfast?"

"We don't normally do breakfast here, George. I could go next door, but I need something more than disposable lighters."

"We were in the same cell once. Forget where. Coulda been Lynn. He wouldn't shut up. Talked all night about some woman. Didn't make no sense. Just mostly her name, you know? Man, he was fucked up. This woman was makin' him crazy."

"What did he say about her? Think real hard."

Deemer screwed up his face and thought. Real hard. "He was sayin' . . . that she was dead? Or that he . . . thought she was dead? 'I thought she was dead. I thought she was dead.' " Deemer's voice went up in pitch like he was quoting a child.

"*When* was this?" asked Myles.

Deemer shrugged. "Few months back."

"OK, so what was her name?" Myles continued impatiently.

"I know it if I heard it."

Myles slammed his hand against the bars. "Don't bullshit me, James!"

Deemer didn't flinch. "Gimme some names."

Myles looked at him long and hard. "Alice. Debbie.

Jodie. Julie. Rachel. Adele. Mary. Laura. Sasha. Lola. Vanna. Linda. Moira. Patricia. Susan."

Deemer smiled. "Moira."

The detective stepped back and surveyed him. "So why was that so hard to tell me? Was it painful? Some kind of state secret, Mr. Bush?"

Deemer looked him square in the eye. "Man, ever' time I talk to youse it's painful."

Myles sighed. "How do you like your eggs? You go to court in an hour."

Deemer perked up. "With ketchup. So . . . in court . . . can I choose where I go?"

"No, just your eggs," answered Myles.

Chapter 17

Monday, Monday

Saratoga Computer Systems occupied a building in Centennial Park on Route 128 in the city of Peabody. Route 128 had been renamed America's Technology Highway back when the Massachusetts Miracle was beginning to evolve, and predated Silicon Valley as a greenhouse for the computer industry. Centennial Park had been built in the hopes of drawing the miracle a bit farther north. But now the miracle had washed away, swept out like the tide, leaving expansive office parks throughout the state nearly empty in many cases, so many richly appointed abandoned shells. The few companies that remained had laid off and pulled in to keep from drying out.

Saratoga had survived by cutting back to less than half its peak work force. Throughout most of the onslaught, Sasha Doheny had survived, working in the Quality Assurance department as a member of the test team. The team had been trimmed down to two. But then in early January, three weeks before her sister's death, Sasha was laid off. Quality Assurance at Saratoga became a joke; Sasha Doheny's life became a nightmare.

Working as a part-time word processor, Moira had outlasted the cutbacks, only to be cut down by the increasingly persistent and debilitating head pains she incurred from her car accident. Saratoga accommodated her first by reducing her hours, then by hiring her on a contract basis when her schedule became less predictable.

Late Monday morning and operating on three nonconsecutive hours of sleep, Dunn spoke first to Moira's former manager, then to various employees who knew her best. Moira Doheny had been quiet, but well liked. Quiet about her personal life. Even quieter since her accident. But a sweet girl.

Finally he was led to the word-processing office where the sole remaining word processor made her home. The room was bedecked with posters of men in Jockey shorts, Far-Side cartoons, and warning signs. Getting something typed at Saratoga was about as easy as gaining entrance to a missile base.

Jackie Warden, the single most powerful employee at Saratoga, had barricaded her desk with a row of black plastic bins. Bins for work requests, the work itself, the triplicate request forms, a process which took longer than the actual job. Jackie's hair was moussed into little peaks. Dunn felt he would probably continue typing his own letters.

Jackie knew both of the Doheny sisters well. Part of her job was to know everyone in the company. She typed all their résumés for them at night, knowing who was dissatisfied, who wanted out, who was afraid. She also knew whose jobs were in jeopardy.

"Want some coffee, honey?" Jackie set down a cigarette and reached to refill her mug. On the side of it was one of those "You want it *when?*" cartoons. Dunn looked at the coffee. Then back at her hair. What the hell—life is full of risks. It smelled fresh.

"Thanks, yes. Black, please. Miss Warden . . ."

"Call me Jackie," she ordered.

"Jackie, when did you last see Moira?"

"She came in last week to do some work. She's typing up

a user's manual for one of our products." She poured out the two mugs and handed one to Dunn.

"Did she ever take work home? She had a typewriter."

Jackie looked at him with something that might have passed for patience. "We do everything on word processors. She didn't have one at home."

"How did she seem when she was in? What day was it?"

"Mmmh, OK at first. It was . . ." She turned and flipped through her desk calendar. "Wednesday. She came in Wednesday. Worked a few hours. She went home around three."

"Why? Did she mention any pain?"

"She didn't talk about it. She tried not to. But she didn't look too great when she left." Jackie pulled open a drawer and brought out a green box. "Girl Scout cookie?" she offered.

Dunn declined. "Did she say anything to you about her plans for the rest of the week? Whether she intended to go anywhere or see anyone, like Friday night?"

Jackie pressed her lips together and shook her head. "She was real quiet about her . . . social life."

"Did she ever talk to you about 'escape?' About doing something about the pain? Or about suicide directly?"

Jackie laughed. "Around here? We all do. She never exactly said she would like really take her own life. But she didn't know what to do, she'd be like at wit's end sometimes. A lot of times when it was bad, one of us would drive her home. She'd have to lie down in a dark room all day. The next day, she'd be OK."

Dunn sipped his coffee. Tasted like coffee.

Jackie continued: "Actually, you know, come to think of it, it must have crossed her mind. Sasha got her some pamphlets once from the Hemlock Society, or whatever they're called. That suicide company?"

"When did they tell you this?"

"Oh, they never told me. I saw them on Sasha's desk one night when I was returning a file of hers. About a month ago. Just before she was laid off."

"Did either of them ever bring it up?"

"Nope. Not to me."

Dunn pondered the number of people in the young girl's life who cared for her enough to want her suffering to end. He wondered how many others had written the Hemlock Society on her behalf. *Here's something that might interest you, dear* . . .

Myles groaned. Eugene Sollors was eluding them. So far, he hadn't returned any of the messages they had left with Adele or at his own place. Myles had swung by Sollors's address a half dozen times during the past two days. A neighbor had told him Sollors appeared to come by frequently, though didn't usually stay long. So while Dunn was at Saratoga Monday morning, Myles picked up a box of Munchkins, a large coffee, the newspaper, and his latest book on the Kennedy conspiracy theory, drove back to Sollors's, and settled in for a stakeout. He had also tried reaching Judd Grimes again, to confront him with his obsession with Moira. Judd, too, seemed to be out.

Jake Myles had grown up in Salem, as had Dunn and the majority of the cops in the department. He kept his high school yearbook in his top desk drawer. It contained the pictures of three others on the force, and two faces now doing time. Countless others had been through the station, victimized or victimizing. Myles looked up names in it every day. Looking for some jamoke's first mug shot.

A few months back, Myles had turned thirty. The Big One. Thirty years and still not divorced, an anomaly in the department. Not even married. Still working through all the emergency-room nurses at Salem Hospital. He couldn't shake his addiction to white stockings.

Aside from nurses, when the Celtics weren't playing and softball season hadn't started, Myles spent his time reading true crime paperbacks, and the occasional mystery when real people weren't killing each other in spectacular enough fashion. He knew all of it would pay off when he took the sergeant's exam in the fall.

Before getting down to his studies, Myles dug out a Munchkin, adjusted the radio, then made a couple of calls to Salem Hospital on the car phone to line up a little gratuitous sex for his next night off.

In a nearby mall, Chris Alexei stuck a quarter into the machine and played another game of Tetris, accompanied by frenzied repetitions of a Russian folk song, reduced and arranged for videogame honkytonk and sounding like a Baltic Super Mario Brothers. The East India Mall was a block from the courthouse. The video-game arcade in the mall's food court was as good a place as any to consider events. To pause for thought. To think about his life, his career, his lack of a woman, his loss of a child.

A T-shape came sailing out of the sky. He had a full stanza in which to rotate and align it to maximize his score. Another came drifting down. The music started picking up speed.

His arraignment over, Chris had eight weeks before his trial date and probable conviction. Eight weeks to get his life in order. Close up his apartment. Move some stuff. Clear the calendar. Forward his mail. He positioned an I-beam into a narrow hole. Perfect fit. His score shot up. More shapes rained down.

So what was on the calendar? For starters, Moira's funeral tomorrow, wake today. The music sped up some more. Gaps were forming. Chris was in trouble.

Salem Jail was a hellhole. One of the oldest county jails in the country, it was designed to hold a hundred men, but had been pressed into service for up to two hundred on occasion. "Service" was not quite the right word. The jail was being shut down this year. Chris would probably never walk its tiers again. By the time he went in they were supposed to have moved to the new facility ten miles away in Middleton.

During Chris's first stretch at Salem they had a riot. Every few years the place had needed a good riot. Like a forest fire. Clear out all the underbrush. Hose the place down. All the fixtures would get ripped out. Only way to get 'em replaced down there. Beds would get dismantled, doors, bars, chunks of wall. If it was there, it may as well be somewhere else.

Only thing that didn't get touched, not so much as a scratch, was the bank of pay phones down on the lowest tier. Like a row of shrines. The telephone line was your lifeline. And a broken phone didn't get repaired too quickly. An inmate making a call couldn't jiggle a stuck coin out or slam down a receiver without a hundred and fifty pairs of eyes boring into his back. Guys could routinely take steel beds apart with their bare hands and they'd handle the pay phones like they were made of glass.

The last few L's had come down too fast to rotate and piled up end to end, bringing Chris's wall to the top, loosely built and full of holes. The music rebuked him. The screen offered another game. Another chance. Distinguish yourself. Avenge yourself. Just twenty-five cents. Chris jingled the remaining coins in his pocket and stared at the screen. *Boy or girl,* he wondered. The game played itself while waiting for his response. "See how easy it is?" the screen taunted. *Why couldn't she tell me?*

Ken Griffey, Jr., may have had a great batting average, but his card wasn't worth shit. *Ht: 6′3″ Wt: 195 Bats: left Throws: left.* Eugene Sollors put it back and selected a 1957

Topps Bob Clemente worth about two hundred dollars. And a 1971 Pete Rose, going for about forty-five. Just a little lunch money. Don't rush things. Upon reconsideration, however, he pulled out the Satchel Paige. Worth some bucks. He knew a place in Wakefield he could get good prices for them.

Whistling "Take me out to the Ball Game," Sollors slipped the cards inside his jacket pocket and returned the box to its hiding place inside the wall. The garage belonged to a friend of his. A guy with no record. A guy who had given Sollors a key last fall when the weather started getting cold, so he could store his Camaro. Sollors had returned the favor with a nice leather jacket that had come his way. By now the kid had probably forgotten all about the key. No one would trace him here. Sollors replaced the piece of paneling and pushed the work bench back into place.

Actually, he had plenty of lunch money. And noontime was early for Sollors to be up. He patted his jacket pocket and pierced the empty garage with his smile. What he really wanted was to play with his cards.

Chapter 18

The Pealey House

The parking lot outside Saratoga was partially submerged beneath dams of melted snow. Dunn had been unsuccessful in picking an entirely dry path back to the gray car. He wanted to revisit Moira's house, but elected to stop by his own on the way to switch his soggy running shoes for some warm, dry workboots.

From his house, Dunn gave Moira's landlord a call and arranged to meet him over on Moody Street. As he replaced the receiver, Monday's delivery shot through the mail slot. Dunn gathered it up, pulled his jacket back on, and picked his way from house to car, avoiding Roger the dog's landmines. The detective swore aloud. It was a wonder the postman didn't just hurl the mail from the sidewalk. Dunn made it to the car and threw his stack on the front seat.

The Pealey house had been a landmark of sorts in North Salem prior to the death of its owner. Stories of Mr. Pealey's eccentricities could fill volume four of the history of Salem. However, until his demise a decade ago, most went unsubstantiated. After the discovery of his body, three cold days after he breathed his last breath, the pet rat story was found to be true, although the neighbors never had had any doubts. The rats had worked through the supply of kibble Mr. Pealey had laid out for them, and by the third day had worked their way through a portion of Mr. Pealey himself. Exactly which portions was a topic still debated in the far corners of the city ten years later.

Also confirmed was the presence of a makeshift fallout shelter buried in the yard and connected to the house by a tunnel, long since filled in by the Haynes family when they set about rehabilitating the deteriorated property. Word was that the reclusive Pealey didn't require war to be declared to precipitate his frequent flights to the shelter. He regularly dug in for weeks at a time if so much as a Jehovah's Witness knocked on his door.

"Tell me more about the boyfriends you said were coming and going all the time," Dunn asked Haynes as the front door swung open. The landlord glanced around for mail, but none had yet arrived.

"Ran into them last week pulling out of the garage. I let both units use it, but the Reeses, the folks upstairs, they never use it," explained the man.

"What were Moira's friends doing in there?" Dunn asked.

Their story was that they worked on their car in there. Haynes hadn't objected, but told them not to store any flammables around. Dunn's interest grew. It was, of course, quite common for burglars to stash merchandise they didn't unload right away at their girlfriends' places. "Let's take a look in the garage," Dunn suggested.

As they crunched down the driveway, the detective asked about the famous fallout shelter. "It was right below here," said the landlord. "You can see where the vents used to be—those square patches in the cement."

"Is the shelter still there?"

"I think so. My brother was the one doing the work

here. Mr. Pealey, he stored his garbage in there when the cars filled up."

"Cars?" asked Dunn.

"He had a couple cars out back here, used to put his garbage in there. And his rats when they died. He'd leave 'em in there during the winter until the ground softened up and he could bury 'em proper."

"Right," said Dunn. He thought about his own father, nearing seventy. And about what he would do when Dad started saving little rat corpses till springtime. "So can we see the shelter?"

"Well, the tunnel from the cellar got bricked up when they shored up the foundation. Took a lot of work, this place. But there may have been a way in from the garage."

The garage looked like it had once been a barn or carriage house, itself badly in need of shoring up. Inside, there was evidence that someone had started to clear it out, then had given up. The interior still housed a hangar's worth of potential landfill material. Haynes led the way in. "We're still tidying a bit," he explained.

"Takes time," sympathized the detective.

It was one of those old-fashioned places with a board-covered pit in the middle to stand in while working on cars, when they were invented. The two men lifted up a few of the planks. Mr. Haynes came up with a short ladder and Dunn climbed down inside.

Illuminated by his streamlight, the pit consisted of field-stone and cement, with a crude hollow at one end filled with bags of garbage. Dunn pulled out a few of the bags and poked the light in behind them. The back of the hollow appeared to be wood, not cement. Three vertical two by eights, about four feet high, were wedged into the rough rock. Dunn fished for his Swiss Army knife and teased out the middle plank. Cold, moist air greeted him, with a hollowness he could smell. The hairs on the back of his neck stirred. The detective smiled. "I feel like Nancy Drew," he said.

"What's that?" asked Haynes from the edge of the pit.

"Forget it. Come on down," answered Dunn.

Dunn pulled out the other two planks and ducked through the opening. One steep step down brought him into a concrete tunnel with a slightly vaulted ceiling. Rust and ice crystals were caught in the beam of his light. Green lichen hung in patches like shredded wallpaper. Reinforcement cables, chicken wire, nailers, and light sockets testified to the seriousness of the tunnel's original purpose. Dunn followed it toward the house, where it ended in a wall of cinder blocks, permanently sealed off.

A side passage led to the bomb shelter, a small, claustrophobic room with a dysfunctional light fixture in the ceiling, a rotting camping table in the center, and on the floor a half box of army rations—cans of water and fruit cocktail, by the labels. Dunn felt that life in this shelter, even for a few weeks, would be a poor second to standing in the vicinity of ground zero above.

No signs of stolen merchandise. The room had been cleaned up pretty well, apparently. Dunn traveled around the perimeter, working every inch with his light. Signs indicated he was not the only recent visitor, judging by disturbances in the dust on the table and fresh scrapes on the damp rock floor.

Mr. Haynes had stayed out in the tunnel. As Dunn rejoined him, the streamlight picked up what at first appeared to be a garden snake beside the step up to the pit. When the detective bent down for a closer look, he found instead an electrical cord, new, still folded up and tied in the middle. Looked like it went to a boom box or small appliance. Probably not traceable, but certainly suggestive.

This was a storybook hiding place for someone's hot merchandise. And hide, they had.

On his return from North Salem, Dunn pulled into one of the CID spots on Central Street in front of the station and killed the engine. As he opened the door, he reached for the stack of mail on the seat beside him. It was at that moment that he noticed the birthday card to his sister, under the YMCA flyer and electric bill. Dunn swore as he pulled it out. Then he caught the address. Rachel Carlson. 93 Broad St. Salem, Mass. 01970. *No such number,* the post office announced, with a little pointing finger of blame stamped on the front.

Rachel Carlson lived at thirty-nine. Dunn had struck out.

Chapter 19

Sunny Days

Someone matching Eugene Sollors's description pulled up in a black Camaro in front of the apartment on Lafayette. Dude looked like a million bucks. "OK, friend," said Myles softly and put down his book. He glanced at his watch. It was two-thirty P.M. "Time to make the donuts," he muttered, got out of the car, and stepped across the street. "Mr. Sollors, I presume?" he sang out.

Sollors waited for Myles to flash the tin before answering. "Yeah, that's me."

"I'd like to talk to you about Moira Doheny."

"Chris's girl?" asked Sollors. "The one killed herself?"

"That's what I wanna talk about. Can we go inside?"

Sollors locked his car and, carrying a bag of groceries in one arm, led Myles into his apartment. He gestured toward a chair. Sollors unpacked while Myles took a good look around. "Personal stuff's in the drawer by the couch," he said from the kitchen. He knew cops loved to snoop.

On the wall by the TV was a framed trio of baseball cards. Myles could make out Pete Rose in the middle. "You a collector?" he asked.

"Since I was a kid," answered Sollors, stowing a bottle of juice in the refrigerator.

Myles found the parakeets. "What's these?" he called

out. "It's a fucking job requirement for thieves to have little pets at home?"

"I am not a thief," announced Sollors from the doorway.

"Gene. I read your résumé. Don't try and shit me. Now do these eat their young?"

"My name's Eugene. They eat Hartz Mountain Budgie food."

Myles smiled. *"Eu* . . . gene. There's a song about that. When did you last see Moira?"

Sollors frowned. "She was Chris's girl, not mine."

"When did *you* last see her?"

The boy shrugged. He had hair like a surfer's. A good tan for January. "It's probably been a few weeks."

"So how long were you in for?" asked Myles, pawing through the magazines on the floor.

Sollors laughed a golden, easy laugh. "That was years ago, man. Another life. I work now. Clean living. File a fucking *tax* return, pal. I'm one of your employers." His smile would have sent the Marlboro man packing.

Myles grinned. He didn't bother asking about his work. It would be free lance, whatever it was. And between jobs. "So tell me about Chris and Moira," he asked instead.

"Chris and Moira. Well, it's no secret they were kind of splitting up," said Sollors, finally sitting down. "Moira wanted Chris to go straight. He couldn't. He's one of those kids who's like addicted to crime."

"But . . . ah . . . you could? Go straight?"

"I just outgrew it. I went to all the programs in jail. I saw the light." He dazzled the room with his teeth again. "I've tried to help Chris turn it around."

You're full of shit, thought Myles. "You have?" he asked.

"I bailed him out, Saturday."

"Do you think he killed Moira?" asked the detective.

"Chris? Jeez. Well, no. I think she did commit suicide."

Myles stretched out his legs. "She ever talk to you about it?"

"She talked to a lot of people about it, I thought. Not saying she'd do it exactly, but it definitely crossed her mind, I'd say."

"Why do you think she chose a gun instead of pills?" asked Myles, studying Sollors.

"Why? Well, Moira didn't know much about drugs except what her doctor told her. She was a pretty innocent kid, you know. Trying to kill yourself with pills—it's easy to mess up. You don't take enough, or you throw up, where does that leave you? Damaged. A gun's safer."

"Where did she get the gun? Do you know?"

Sollors leaned back. "Chris gave it to her. Long time ago. For protection. Turned out it was a bad idea, wasn't it?"

Myles nodded. The police had traced the gun to a man in Ipswich who had reported it stolen from his store in mid-1989. If Sollors was telling the truth, Ipswich police would be interested in talking to Chris.

"So, where were you Friday night, Saturday morning?" Myles asked.

Sollors gave him a small smile. "Giving Adele Prada a night to remember."

Myles took out his notebook and a pencil. "You want to elaborate, Gene?"

"My name's Eugene" came the answer. "We were fucking like minks."

"Feeling better?" Dunn had risked a phone call to his sister, unsure of what he would unleash. Trinidad had brought in coffees and was screwing around with the copy machine.

"No. Worse." Rachel gave a long sigh. "I'm twenty-six years old and I'm tired. Is this what life is?"

"Life with young kids, Rachel. If you can call it that."
He dropped the plastic lid into his wastebasket and blew
on his first sip.

"Buster and Lenny were sent home from day care. The
staff found nits on their heads. Gabe, we've been battling
head lice for the past two weeks. We buy Kwell shampoo
by the six-pack. The teachers look at me like I'm guilty of
germ warfare. Like I'm trying to slip little human bombs
into their school. My friends treat me like a leper. I can't
get a sitter, no surprise there. I'm missing work again, Warren can't get off today, and I need the kids out of here so I
can burn the house down. What do I do? Take them out
and tie them to a tree? How about you come and arrest
them? Take them away from their unfit parents."

"OK. Shall we release them for adoption?"

"Only if someone bails them out. How soon can you be
here?"

"As soon as I get the warrants." The detective hung up.

Dunn dug through the cupboard below the copier and
fished out one of the police department gas masks. In Salem's three-hundred-sixty-year history, law enforcement
had yet to find a use for them. The day war was declared in
the Persian Gulf, Jake Myles had worn one to Brodie's
Pub on a bet. Anything to enhance the department's public image.

At Rachel's front door, Dunn pressed the bell and
slipped on the mask. Buster Carlson, aged five, opened the
door and screamed. His younger brother, crouching behind him, let out a deep belly laugh.

"Buster, lighten up," Dunn said, in a voice sounding like
Darth Vader's.

Rachel appeared in the basement doorway with a pile of
sheets. "Get your coats on, kids. You're going to jail with
Uncle Gabe."

Dunn lifted the mask. "What the hell's that noise?"

"The dryer?" she offered.

"No. Upstairs. Sounds like a subway train," he said.

Rachel answered: "Oh. The rock tumbler."

"The what?" Dunn repeated.

"Rock tumbler. The boys and their dad gave it to me for my birthday. It, uh, tumbles rocks around to make them better." She looked like she hadn't slept in five years.

"Great gift!" He said to the kids. "Sounds like a *subway train!*" He bent down and helped them into a matched set of green Celtics jackets. The younger one, Lenny, gathered up a day's supply of Ninja Turtles. Rachel followed them out into the front yard.

"Where's your Chevy?" she asked.

"Are you kidding? I don't want crab lice in my car. I brought a cruiser."

"They're not crab lice. They're head lice."

"Just the same, I'll have to pat them down."

Dunn frisked the kids and stuck them into the backseat, where after a few minutes of digging, he located working sets of seat belts. As he shut the door, the detective reached into his jacket, pulled out Rachel's birthday card, and laid it on the sheets in her arms.

Chapter 20

Losing You

Monday afternoon visiting hours for Moira Doheny were nearly over. Chris hesitated outside the funeral home before going in. Obligation propelled him forward, finally, though dread slowed his pace. Moira had tried to socialize him once. To teach him how to behave in the civilized world. Protocol was not his bag. But he owed it to Moira to say a proper goodbye, whatever that meant.

Beside the casket, members of the family were seated on folding chairs. A couple of vases filled with white flowers stood to one side. The last of her visitors spoke in quiet tones, some glancing at watches. Chris's discomfort increased. He disliked crowds, even small ones. For Chris, two was a crowd.

Steeling himself, he went up to the family and extended his hand. "I'm very sorry," he mumbled, starting with who obviously was Moira's father. Mr. Doheny answered mechanically, without looking up higher than Chris's waist. Sasha, however, studied his face with uncertain recognition until at last he spoke. "My name's Chris. I was a friend . . ."

"Oh, yes, Chris. I think we met." She worked her brow. "Where was it—last spring? The hospital, maybe?"

Chris shook his head. "I don't think so. I wasn't able . . . to get over there." Since the Willie Horton case, furloughs were tough in Massachusetts. Moira had not been hurt enough or related enough for an exception to be made in Chris's case. After the hospital, Moira had stayed with Sasha for a while. Chris had called her there a few times from the jail. By the time he was out, Moira was recovering at home.

They had met, once. He knew Sasha would remember, and preferred to be gone when she did. Chris shook hands with a woman who introduced herself as Moira's mother and claimed to know all about him. The implications of this only added to his misery. He stepped to the far side of the casket and knelt on the floor, hoping this posture would protect him from any further social graces. Chris didn't understand how wakes were supposed to work. Or families. If he couldn't take it apart with his hands, it was beyond his comprehension. He studied his reflection in the varnish for a moment, then got up and left the building.

Out in the parking lot, he slipped into his car, a snow-white Corvette; the car he had tried to give Moira last summer. It had been on the day she was returning to work, resigned to the fact that her recovery was as complete as it was going to be. Chris had been out on parole nearly a week, back on the job himself. He had bought the car to replace the one she had totaled. The pleasure of making the purchase was physical and intense, and as addictive as the pleasure of swinging open a safe door. But the thrill of buying it for Moira was the greatest rush of all. In some sense Moira had tamed him. But being tamed left him without natural protection against the winds of human emotion.

That was the moment when he had met Sasha. Moira's sister had come early to give her a lift to Saratoga. When Chris arrived in this glorious machine and attempted to hand Moira the keys, Moira looked at them, looked at the Corvette, then at Chris. Then, inexplicably, she refused him. "No," she said. "No." Sasha had been there, leaning in the doorway as Chris stood in the front yard, stripped naked for all of North Salem to see. Pain so intense the anger was eclipsed. Pain he had in his youth forgotten how to feel, when he learned to live without family he was better off without.

Moira never accepted a thing from him after that, except his affection, and when he could give it, his love.

Chris turned the key in the ignition. The engine responded faithfully and with its usual reliability. He remembered he hadn't said goodbye.

As he headed for the parking lot exit, he slowed the car in front of the ornate front door and hit the window button. When it had lowered he leaned out and whispered, "Hey, Moira." Suddenly the smell of her hair hit him with crippling force. He raised the window and floored the accelerator. *When the singer's gone let the song go on* . . .

At four-thirty Dunn finished his Monday-morning reports, picked up his radio, and called the North Salem car. Now that he knew the latest secrets of the Pealey house, he wanted the beatman to keep an extra eye on it during the night. Officer Frank Mallory was already on his dinner break, a half hour into the shift. But he agreed to swing by a few times. Work it into his busy schedule.

Dunn suspected Mallory wasn't in a restaurant. In addition to a legitimate family in South Salem, the patrolman had an illegitimate one in North Salem. And a couple of extra girlfriends on the beat for emergencies. If Mallory's wife ever reached the breaking point and went on a rampage, a good portion of the North Salem female population could become decimated. The remaining female population, rather.

"I have news, and the prints," announced Myles, striding into the detectives' office. He laid the packet of crime-scene photos on Dunn's desk. "First of all, did you know that before he moved to Dallas, Jack Ruby worked for the FBI?"

"Nope," said Dunn. The copier was out of paper. He slammed a fresh package down on the counter and ripped apart the end. Buster and Lenny were working their way through desk drawers.

Myles continued: "His real name was Rubenstein. But I have more."

"That's good."

Myles glanced at the kids. "Where'd you scoop the muffs?"

"Broad Street," answered Dunn.

"Anyway, take a look at this!" Myles handed him the classified section of Monday's paper. A box in the corner had been circled in red:

St. Jude's Novena

May the Sacred Heart of Jesus be
adored, glorified, loved, and preserved
throughout the world now and forever.
Sacred Heart of Jesus, pray for us. St.
Jude, worker of miracles, pray for us.
Say this prayer 9 times a day, by the
8th day your prayer will be answered.
It has never been known to fail.
Publication must be promised. My
prayers have been answered.
　　　　　　　　　　　　—S.D.

Dunn read it aloud, then looked up at Myles. "What's this got to do with Jack Ruby?"

"Not Jack Ruby, Moira Doheny. Who do you think S.D. is?"

"Nine times eight is seventy-two. I hope the miracle was worth it." Dunn loaded the paper tray and shoved it into place.

"The miracle was *Moira's death!* 'S.D.' is Sasha Doheny!"

"Whoa there, big fella!" Dunn held up one hand and jabbed Start with the other. " 'S.D.' could be anyone. Sammy Davis. Sandra Dee. Scooby Doo." The copier didn't respond. "Sandy Duncan."

"You saw her when she described Moira's head pain. Maybe her motives were good, maybe not so good. But if she was writing to some suicide club, she either wanted Moira to kill herself or wants us to think Moira did. Being that interested, I think she could maybe have helped."

"Helped? Why? You don't think seventy-two novenas were enough to do the trick?" asked Dunn.

"Gabe, it's time we took a look at who stands to gain by Moira's death. Like get a warrant to look at the parents' wills. Maybe Sasha was planning ahead."

"Warrant? I'm not sure a St. Jude's Novena constitutes probable cause. And I didn't get the impression that Sasha was that religious." Dunn jiggled the paper holder.

"You don't have to be religious to pray. Don't you ever pray?"

Dunn responded, "Every day I come to work. But I never promise publication."

"Bet those prayers don't get answered," said Myles.

Dunn hit Reset on the copier, then Continue, then Start. Nothing happened. "You got that right."

Judd Grimes spent the better part of Monday trying to score a couple of lines of coke. Cash was low at present. But he needed to get his head together, and this was the first order of business. Eventually, a woman he knew in the Point came through for him. For fifty dollars he was handed a tightly folded square cut from a glossy magazine cover, filled with enough white powder to get him through the day, he hoped.

Judd did two quick lines in the car, then headed home to Beverly. The bridge was up. Judd sat in growing traffic on the Salem side and shared a collective impatience at sailors and bridge tenders. As his mind cleared, Judd again began to sense that he was in danger. Danger from Adele. The cops would get around to calling her, just like they called him. And then she would figure it out.

He scratched at his tattoo until the bridge lowered.

Chapter 21

We Shall Overcome

Buster wasn't too keen on sharing the stale donut with his brother. "When are we going home?" he asked.

"I don't want to go home," answered Lenny.

Dunn frowned. "I don't know, boys. We went easy on you last time. This time, well, this is what's called your wrap-up bid. We keep you till the end. No parole. You pay your full debt to society. At least until dinner."

"What are they in for?" asked Braedon, who was trying to enter a stolen vehicle into the computer.

Dunn leaned back and parked his feet on his desk. "Harboring nits. Abusive treatment of parents. We're looking at some state time," Dunn answered. "The older one sometimes goes by Buster Crab."

Buster wandered over to Braedon and requested some computer games be put at his disposal. The detective told him all they had was Golf, but he was welcome to sit on his lap and watch him play Stolen Property. After a while, Braedon began to scratch himself. "It was nice of Uncle Gabe to bring you by," he announced.

A layer of phone messages cloaked Dunn's desk like leaves in autumn. He swept some up and triaged them into various aging piles. One stack concerned the break-ins. One for the Doheny case, one for the unknowables, one for the unanswerables. One directly filed in the basket beneath his feet.

Dunn went to work on the first of the slips, a call from the owner of the Sports King. As he dialed, four-year-old Lenny, who had outgrown playing with the bubbler, came over to work on Dunn's shoes. "Leonard, if you tie my laces together I will handcuff you to the copy machine." Then: "Good afternoon, is Mr. Lazarus available? This is Gabe Dunn, Salem Police."

Mr. Lazarus had called earlier to say a baseball dealer he knew well in Wakefield had turned down a kid trying to sell a signed Satchel Paige card earlier in the afternoon. The dealer thought it looked like one of Lazarus's, by the color of the ink. He had attempted to stall the seller, but the kid spooked and split. Dunn took down the dealer's name and number. "Will most dealers recognize the card?" Dunn asked.

"Yes, Sergeant, they will. Unfortunately, few of them will report it nowadays. This one was a friend."

Dunn told him the police had circulated descriptions of the most valuable cards to dealers throughout New England, and had faxed copies to other police departments in the area. Mr. Lazarus thanked him, but his voice held little hope.

There was no answer when the detective dialed Lazarus's friend. As he listened to the ringing, Dunn pulled the yellow envelope from Essex Camera toward him and opened it up. Pictures of Moira and her living room in crisp detail and breathtaking color, larger than life, brighter than memory. Myles was good. He should do wedding pictures.

The camera had captured it all. The note, the typewriter, the butt of the gun showing the serial number. The bullet from the wall. The shells in the desk. The edges of every door. No tool marks on the locks. Interior of the medicine cabinet. A few views of the living room, a half dozen of Moira, red hair made brilliant by the flash, ivory skin, paisley robe, dark-green rug. Like a window display at Landry and Arcari Interiors.

Often the camera discovers details which were overlooked at the scene. Flash photos made the pool of blood more discernible against the dark-green pile, and had illuminated, much to Dunn's annoyance, a disturbance in the edge—a smearing of some sort. The nearly dry puddle had been obvious at the scene, the boundaries had not. Now, clearly, Dunn could see the effects of untrained observers, contaminating and compromising his scene even before his arrival. Someone—the landlord, the patrolman, Myles, or any of the dozen officers and patrol supervisors who had dropped by—all dutifully recorded in the patrolman's notebook, someone had stepped in Moira's blood. Dunn was pissed.

He scribbled a note to Detective Sheila Tobias on Lazarus's lead, got up, nearly stepping on his nephew, and laid the break-in file on Sheila's desk. Lenny was studying the pile of gravel he had picked out of Dunn's soles. The policeman bent down to retie his laces.

"When's this big guy start school?" asked Braedon, letting Buster slide off his lap. Dunn was holding out jackets. "When's he gonna become another brick in the wall?"

"You start first grade next year, Buster?" asked Dunn. The kid nodded. The detective reached for Lenny's arms and began to stuff them into their Celtics sleeves. Lenny's hands felt like Brillo pads. When the first fist projected through its cuff, Dunn pried open the fingers and brushed off the residue from the streets of Salem. The second fist emerged. Opening it like a clam shell, the detective found contained within a bright-orange sticker, stuck to the tip of

Lenny's index finger. He picked it off and was about to toss it when he noticed the printing.

Sports King. $899.

Rachel transferred the last of the sheets to the dryer and set it on high for forty-five minutes. *Fry, you little bastards.* Back upstairs she zipped up her jacket, turned on the vacuum, and attacked the living room. The house had never been so clean. She emptied her third can of spray along the top of the sofa. *Drown, you suckers.* Every window was open, bringing the house down to about fifty degrees. Rachel had carried pillows, cushions, and stuffed animals outside. She had pounded and turned mattresses, exposing every exposable surface in the house to the winter's fury. And to her own. *Freeze, assholes.*

In a household as rambling and chaotic as hers, purging the lice was no easy feat. All the brochures reassured patients that "Pediculosis is not a sign of being dirty. It strikes rich and poor alike . . ." *Can't prove it by us.* Rachel knew one thing: she couldn't accuse the boys of sharing combs.

By the time the gray, unmarked cruiser pulled back into the driveway, it was close to six and Rachel had reclaimed her house. Her energy level had risen, her face flushed, her revenge sweet. Stepping outside to greet her sons, she stretched her arms out. *"We are the champions!"* she sang out.

As the kids raced in to reinfect their home, Dunn leaned against the car and shoved his hands in his pockets. In the darkness his face was illuminated by the porch light. Rachel walked over and kissed him. "Thanks," she said quietly.

Dunn smiled. "Anytime. Everything OK now?"

She pulled her jacket tightly around her. "I won the battle. There's still the war."

Dunn put his arm around her shoulders. "What war, Rachel? What is it you want?"

His sister didn't answer. Whatever her war, it remained undeclared. After a while she asked: "How's your job?"

"Your little one dug up a clue for me in one of my cases. Or might of. Have you bought anything recently from a place called Sports King? He sells sports collectibles. You know, baseball cards and stuff."

She managed a smile. "You mean with gum and everything?"

Dunn continued: "Well, some have gum. I'm interested in an item that went for eight hundred and ninety-nine dollars. I don't know if it came with gum."

"I would hope for eight hundred ninety-nine dollars you get something. But sorry, we get our sports collectibles out of the Wheaties boxes. Saves us eight hundred and ninety-six dollars."

"I figured it was out of your price range. I just wanted to be sure. Lenny had the price sticker on his finger. I think it's from a break-in at the store last Thursday night."

Rachel frowned. "Well, I wouldn't put it past him, but he was in front of the TV last Thursday night."

"I'm relieved to hear that. Actually, I think he picked it off my shoe today, so I could have picked it up during the investigation Friday." He paused.

"I'd invite you in, but it's warmer out here," said his sister.

"You couldn't pay me to go in there. Not until the Board of Health rules it safe," he answered. "As I think about it, Rachel, I wasn't wearing these shoes when we went to the scene."

"How do you remember what shoes you wore last week?"

Dunn began to pace. Patches of slushy snow in the driveway gave way beneath his feet. He usually wore these

workboots on snowy days. Salem hadn't had a deep snow-
fall in nearly two weeks. His Reeboks had sufficed through
the recent layers, until this morning's onslaught in the Saratoga parking lot. "I stopped home late this morning to
put these on. They still had newspapers in them from being soaked a couple of weeks ago. So where did I walk
today after that?"

Buster Carlson leaned out of the upstairs kitchen window and aimed a green plastic Ping-Pong gun at his uncle.
At the sound of the plock, Dunn clutched his chest. "Re-
cidivist!" he gasped. He staggered to the cruiser door and
yanked it open. "Call me when they're in college," he
shouted as he started up the engine.

"So what's the answer?" Rachel yelled.

"Moira Doheny's garage. I think Lenny's cracked the
Sports King job."

Chapter 22

The Woman in Me

Detective Sheila Tobias was a good cop, good mother, good wife. She did volunteer work in the community, and paid regular visits to her grandfather's nursing home. Tobias lived on five hours sleep a night, accommodating to a two-year-old's circadian rhythm and sleep habits more bat-like than humanoid. While other cops worked private details or scrabbled for court time, Sheila Tobias sat in pediatricians' waiting rooms holding Tonka trucks. Despite her perpetual sleep deprivation and tenuous management of that special mental state that only working mothers share, Tobias was gradually being recognized as one of the better detectives in the department. Grudgingly recognized. Tobias was new. Her selection over others with greater seniority was a sore spot in various sectors of the uniformed division. But the rest of the CID stuck up for her. They gave her shit cases, but they stuck up for her.

Tobias opened her new file folder on the Witch's Brew burglary. Inside were the officer's report, crime report, and a single sheet of lined paper with some initial notes and phone numbers Billy Trinidad had made. The case was now hers.

The "Brew," as it was known locally, was a pub down on Derby Street near the wharves. The establishment's alarm had gone off about an hour after closing, early Monday. A

little over twelve hundred dollars in cash and some endorsed checks were missing from the crudely peeled safe.
The TV had been yanked from the wall. Some signed dol-
lar bills had been ripped off the mirror—"good luck" bills,
the owner had called them. A bottle of VSOP Hennessy
was sitting out on the bar, but had been left behind. The
backdoor had been forced open from the inside, leading
Trinidad to surmise that the thief had hidden inside at
closing time. Probably in the basement. No useful prints
were found.

Dunn had given her the files on all the B&Es from the
past couple of weeks. Tobias began sifting through them,
nine in all. Three had resulted in arrests. The remaining
six, plus this latest one, awaited her superwoman skills to
reach their resolution. Reaching for a fresh pad of paper,
Tobias started on the phone calls.

Four no-answers, one busy signal, two no-cooperations
later, Detective Tobias pushed the phone away and picked
up one of the Smurfs she kept on her windowsill. *A beautiful day in the neighborhood* . . . She was a good neighbor
and a good citizen. But in between the thin lines she
walked, there were moments when she didn't know who
the hell she was anymore.

The phone rang beside her, an incoming call on the
"Hello" line. "Hello?" she answered. The regular line,
they answered, "Detectives." It was Dunn suggesting that
they bring in Chris Alexei for questioning on the Sports
King case.

Sasha Doheny had stuffed a large Lechmere bag into
the outside pocket of her purse. She stood by Dunn's desk
early Monday evening, having declined a seat. She was
beginning to feel hot in her coat. The office was over-
heated, except by each window where ice formed on your
coffee inside of five minutes.

"My father's worried about her stuff, leaving it there in an empty apartment. I told him I'd try and get you know, personal things, like letters and pictures. Her jewelry. Some of it's my mother's. I tried calling her landlord but I just got his machine. The police aren't guarding it, are they?"

"Afraid not. We're done in there. You and your father can take whatever you want. There shouldn't be a problem with Mr. Haynes. The rent was paid up."

"I don't have a key."

Dunn reached into the Doheny evidence file by his feet and fished out Moira's set of keys. "Tell you what. Why don't I run you over there? On the way you can tell me about the Hemlock Society."

Sasha blanched.

Chris grabbed for the phone on the fifth ring. He set down his keys and bags and reached for the kitchen light. "Chris?" It was Adele. "I wanted to know how your arraignment went."

"It went."

"What happened?" she asked.

"I go back in two months. Judd's pretrial is in six weeks, but I think he's working something out. I was his ride out, of course." With his free hand he unpacked a fresh set of crowbars from the Somerville Lumber bag. Assorted sizes; cheapest ones they had—crowbars all break in the end anyway. Save the quality for your screwdrivers.

"Yeah, well, speaking of Judd, I want to talk to you. Maybe I could come over?"

Chris sounded uncertain. "OK, I guess. But not for long. I'm tired." He hung up.

Chapter 23

Revelations

Dunn opened the car door for Sasha. He went around to the driver's side and got in.

"The pamphlets weren't for Moira," she said when he had shut the door.

"Oh? You considering suicide?" Dunn asked. He started up the engine and turned down the music.

"Suicide's against the law, right?"

"Actually, it's not. We usually try to intervene. Get the person whatever help they need."

She looked out the window. "I can't tell you. They were for someone else."

Dunn was quiet until they turned onto North Street. Then he remembered: "Your father said Saturday he had a brother living in pain. Your uncle? Was that who, Sasha?"

The young woman waited a few blocks. Finally she spoke. "He has cancer. They can't do anything more for him. The literature said 'Good Life, Good Death.' I believe in that. You won't try to contact him, or anything will you? He doesn't want anybody to know . . ."

"I'm not going to bother your uncle. He hasn't committed a crime. You haven't, either, as far as I know. But I'd be real careful how much further you helped your uncle in whatever he's cooking up."

Dunn turned onto Moody. Across from the Pealey

place, he switched off the motor. The street was dark and quiet. The only sounds came from traffic on North Street. They sat for a moment.

"Killing yourself takes courage, doesn't it?" said Sasha.

"So does not killing yourself," answered Dunn.

She turned to him. "You don't think it can be justified sometimes?"

Dunn hesitated. "Personally, yes, I think it can. It depends on what your options are, I guess. Everyone's misery is different. No one else can know how much pain another person can bear."

"Do you think my sister killed herself?" she asked.

"I haven't been convinced yet. Her pain wasn't constant. She had a whole life ahead of her."

"But you said yourself, we can't know other people's pain."

"Right. We *can't* know. But in my job we have to guess."

Sasha looked out the window. "When Moira went into the ditch last spring, I wondered . . . well, it occurred to me it might have been on purpose."

Dunn looked surprised. "I don't understand. She wasn't having headaches before the accident, was she?"

"No. Not . . . physical pain. She never talked to me much about her friends, even about her boyfriend. But enough for me to figure out they were bad news. I told you Moira was the type who thought she could change people. But I think they were changing her. I think she was doing things she couldn't talk about, they bothered her so much. Something in that life was . . . seducing her. And she was finding it hard to pull away. She was, well, ashamed. Of them, and of herself. And she could only get part-time work. That didn't help. My job was shaky, even before I was laid off. My salary was cut—I didn't have a lot to give her."

"Why couldn't she pull away?" asked Dunn.

"You can walk away from friends if you have to, but you can't walk away from yourself."

Dunn looked skeptical. "Sasha, isn't this mostly conjecture? You said she didn't talk much about it."

"But you know, she was always like that as a kid. She'd try so hard at things, and be devastated when they didn't work out. She was always trying to walk away from herself." Her eyes were wet, glistening with reflected street lights.

Ever read Camoo? Dunn thought about asking.

Dunn knew a lot of bad guys who were, in some sense, happy. And good guys who were not. It wasn't the height of your ideals that mattered, but the disparity between your ideals and your self-perception. But twenty-two was too young to give up on yourself. Even when you're good and discover your capacity for bad. Even when times were tough and finding work was much harder than finding despair.

It looked like a big fishing knife. In the dim light of his living room, Judd Grimes's mollies scuttled around in anticipation. The blade a good eight inches, with some inscription, Spanish, he thought. Something about "tuna" visible through the dirt and rust, which proved it was for fishing. The tip of the handle formed a head of an eagle, with a hole in the beak for a chain, or thong, or in this case, a bread-bag wire imprinted THURS THURS THURS. Judd dug out a can of polishing compound and pulled a stool up to his bar. He always meant to clean it up. Probably an antique.

He and Chris had done a job together a year and a half ago. They had made off with a lock box filled with goodies. Chris got his gun then, the Bulldog. Judd had settled for the knife. Burglars didn't usually carry guns anyway. Especially ones with Judd's enviable build. Even scrawny Chris never used one. But the knife had come in handy. It would come in handy now. Just wanted to be cleaned. As he worked the rag, spidery letters revealed themselves.

Me he de comer esa tuna, aungue me espine la mano.

Adele sat across from Chris and stirred her cup of instant coffee. Chris had chugged half a quart of milk down, washing down a few aspirin in the process. He brushed aside tired, dark strands of hair from his forehead.

She began: "I found out something interesting today. Half found out, half figured it out . . ."

"What?" He leaned back and looked at her. She flushed slightly.

Why don't men know how to carry on a simple conversation? "I was going to explain. The cops came by yesterday. Some detective."

"Did you give him my name?" Chris interrupted. Adele could get on his nerves even before she opened her mouth. From then on it was downhill.

"No, well yes, but that's not . . ."

"Thanks, Adele." Chris stood up and opened the refrigerator door. He put the half-empty milk in and took out a beer.

"Chris, they would have connected you sooner or later, you know that. If we tried to hide you now, it would've been more suspicious later."

"We? Was Eugene there?" he demanded.

"No. I don't know if they've talked to him yet," she said.

"I thought not. Eugene wouldn't have given them my name. Just you and Judd." He finished staring into the fridge and slammed the door shut.

Adele fought back tears. "Don't you ever say my name and Judd's in the same breath. I would never do to you the things Judd has done to you," she spat out.

He looked at her. "What things?" he said quietly.

"For starters," she took a breath, "Judd was driving Moira's car the night of the accident. He had had a lot to drink . . ."

When he realized what she was saying, Chris reached for his jacket on the floor next to the kitchen table. *"Sonof-aBITCH!"* he muttered. Then with one booted foot, he kicked open the back door and fled out into the night.

Chapter 24

The Witch's Brew

Sheila Tobias was unable to locate Chris Alexei Monday evening. The detective tried the owner of the Witch's Brew again, successfully this time. Mr. Panakio agreed to meet her down at the bar around eight P.M.

Change does not come lightly to old neighborhoods. And neighborhoods have a way of becoming old at the first sign of change. In the fall of 1987 the Derby Street Café was sold and under its new ownership the name was altered to the Witch's Brew Café. The new owners also replaced the Formica bar with a wooden one, and shifted some of the tables around a little. Just as it had thirty-five years earlier, when the bar had undergone the last in a succession of three hundred years of minor modifications, the neighborhood that patronized the bar by night, complained by day. The new name was a sensitive issue for some people, and for the rest, well, you don't mess with Formica.

In its heyday, Derby Street had been lined with bars, from back when the harbor had been active and entertainment choices had been sparse. Dormant during Prohibition, they sprang forth again in 1933 like weeds between bricks. Now with the waning of the heavy-drinking era, most of them had died out. Only three or so remained, preserved by some kind of sociological natural selection process. The corner of Derby and Daniels had been one of the lucky spots. Since the invention of firewater, barrooms on this corner had been servicing local carpenters, politicians, city workers, and sailors. For foreign mariners docking across the road, the Witch's Brew in all its reincarnations was America. It was also, for three or four nights, home.

Mr. Panakio was fifteen minutes late. Tobias waited at the end of the bar nursing a cup of coffee and listening to a young British sailor wearing a "Salem—Drop by for a Spell" T-shirt and loudly defending the monarchy. Prince Philip was a very nice guy. Princess Di was actually very intelligent. The royal family was the most respected assemblage of human beings in the entire world. Except, apparently, in Salem. Reinforced only with beer, the man was meeting more resistance than Colonel Leslie had.

As he took a seat beside Tobias, Panakio, by way of apology, ordered her up a plate of mushrooms stuffed with crabmeat. She refused a beer. In a heavy Greek accent, the man launched immediately into the story of the break-in. Not very much of a story, actually. Princess Di's intelligence competed seriously for Tobias's attention. The saddest part of the Witch's Brew case had been the loss of the TV.

"You know, it breaks my heart. The neighbors gave me some trouble in the beginning, and I fought the licensing board over a year to get the permit for the TV above the bar. The entertainment license. Harder than the liquor license. In the end I got it. Now they've stolen it from me. Is this not ironic?"

Tobias nodded. "That's very sad," she said. "I'd like to look around downstairs, if I could."

Panakio led her down to the basement. The first room housed refrigerators, freezers, kegs of beer, boxes of placemats and toilet paper. Shelves of ketchup, restaurant sizes of canned goods, racks of wine. They pushed their way through to the back room, which was two steps farther down, and poorly lit. This would have been Tobias's choice for a hiding place. Stacked along walls of fieldstone and punky timbers were the Formica tables of yesteryear. Forests of vinyl-upholstered stools, crates, boxes of Christmas decorations, and a rusted-out steam table provided ample cover during any cursory sweep they might make after the bar was closed up. Ali Baba and forty-odd thieves would have been safe down here.

Tobias borrowed a flashlight and poked around where the ceiling light couldn't reach. She found the work glove immediately, behind the first row of stools. "This yours?" she asked Panakio, picking it up by the thumb.

He studied the brown cotton glove. "No, I don't believe so. I'll check with my people."

Tobias scanned the rest of the basement. Nothing else looked recent. No gum wrappers, no butts. No major rat turds.

"Could I talk to whoever was working last night?"

"Dover. She's upstairs now," said Panakio. They headed back up to the bar.

Tobias had recognized the barmaid earlier. But the latter had apparently not placed Tobias. Dover Landry, a dark-haired woman in her twenties, was a friend of Gabe Dunn's, and had been by the office a couple of times. The woman had been involved in a homicide case the previous year, just before Tobias had joined the CID. Apparently, Dover had believed that the murdered Salem man had been her father. During the late spring, after the case was closed, Dunn had returned with the girl to her home in New Hampshire for a few days to help her sort things out. What exactly was meant by "sorting things out" was the overwhelming topic of conversation in the detectives' office during Tobias's first days on the job, coinciding with Dunn's absence. Dover's build, Dunn's age, the true nature of the journey, all were hotly discussed to the point that Tobias almost asked for her uniform back.

When Dunn returned from New Hampshire, word got out that Dover's biological father had actually been the restaurant owner where her mother had worked until her death. It had been one of those single, brief episodes of consolation, subsequently forgotten, except in the memory of one co-worker. Consolation over a lover's abandonment; the consoler succeeded where the lover had not. Now, mother and lover were dead.

The young woman had made two decisions: not to contact the man, who lived in Center Ossipee with his family, and to return to Massachusetts, the better to forge a life from the future, not the past. The future ended up being Salem, specifically the Witch's Brew. Tobias wondered if Dover had hoped the future would include Dunn. If so, the girl had been disappointed.

When Panakio introduced them, recognition kindled in Dover's eyes. Tobias was sorely tempted to ask on behalf of the department, *So, did you sleep with him?* Instead, she held up the glove like a dead fish. "This yours?" she asked.

Dover Landry, fatherless child, shook her head.

"Any chance you remember anyone last night who might not have left the establishment? Or who behaved in an unusual manner?" Tobias asked.

Dover gave it some thought before answering. "No. It was pretty busy—I don't notice who leaves or doesn't leave. And they all behave in an unusual manner. This crowd, they're from the Willows, mostly." She squirted some soda water into a glass of ice.

"Could someone go downstairs during the evening without you noticing?"

"Sure. The stairs are back by the men's room. Guys go back there all the time."

"Do you check all the basement rooms when you lock up?" asked Tobias.

Dover shook her head. "Not really, no."

Panakio interjected: "We will from now on. And you won't believe the splendid alarm system I ordered today."

Tobias gave him a sympathetic smile, then looked back at Dover. She tried one more question: "Dover, did you by any chance notice if any of your customers were wearing gloves? Gloves like this?"

Dover gave her a disbelieving look. "In a bar? No," she replied in a tone that questioned Tobias's competence.

Tobias smiled at her. *Pretty useless, young lady. No wonder you didn't get him.*

One of the regulars was offering to take the Brit, no longer in condition to walk upright, back to his ship. Detective Tobias packed up her notebook and thanked Mr. Panakio. "I like what you do with your mushrooms," she said.

Chapter 25

Stealing Home

Dunn swung open the door to Moira's apartment and stepped back to let Sasha in. He paused a moment, filling his lungs with the fresh night air. Air cold, damp, and salty, but underneath its numbness, Dunn could still smell leather.

Inside, he flipped on the lights. Nothing appeared to have been disturbed in the forty-eight hours since he had last left it. Sasha stood for a moment in the hallway, afraid to go farther. Dunn shut the door behind them. "It's OK," he said to her. She looked like she was afraid of more shots. "No, wait a second," he said quickly. "Wait right here." He slipped into the kitchen and pulled out a large black trash bag from a box under the sink. Taking it into the living room, the detective spread it carefully over the blood stain on the rug. He moved the desk chair over to secure it. Then he returned to the hall.

Sasha had shifted her gaze to the floor. She was standing in a pile of mail. "What do we do with all this?" she asked. The mail was fresh. Still alive. Untainted, unspattered with Moira's death.

Dunn bent down and collected it. "I look through it, with the family's permission."

"What if we said no?" She was trying to make conversation. Whistling in the dark.

"I have to get a warrant." He continued gathering. Most of it junk. Unforwardable. No forward address anyway.

"Well, be my guest. Take it. Except anything from Ed McMahon." Sasha turned to study the walls. With a puzzled look she announced: "Her pictures and stuff are gone."

Dunn was only half listening, flipping through the rest of the mail. "How so?"

Sasha walked down the hall and back, ducking her head in the kitchen and bedroom before returning. "Just that the place looks so bare and cold. I guess she mentioned a few weeks ago she was getting rid of stuff she didn't need. I haven't been here in a while. She really cleaned out the place. Even some of the furniture." She looked at Dunn. "Down to the bare essentials, huh?"

Dunn asked without looking up: "Did she say anything to you about why?" But Sasha didn't answer.

Dunn had located two personal letters. One from the mother, Iris Perlmutter, postmarked Los Angeles, California. The other was a heavy red envelope, the size of a greeting card. Addressed to Sasha on Pickman Street. Stamped *Insufficient Postage* and returned to the sender. The sender, in the upper left corner, was Moira. The post office always canceled what stamps you had, even when they were refusing to honor them. She started out seventeen cents shy, now she was the whole seventy-five short.

Dunn hefted the card, or whatever it was. The cancellation was Saturday's date, the day Moira died. "May I?" He looked at Sasha, who was afraid to touch it. She nodded vigorously.

Dunn led the way into the living room and turned on the desk lamp. He pulled out his Swiss Army knife and slit open one end of the envelope, then gingerly let the contents slide out onto the desk. A sheet of note paper was wrapped around a flat bundle. The detective lifted open the note with his blade. To Sasha it said in neatly typed lines:

Sash:
These should take care of the car with enough change for sheepskin seat covers.

love—M

PS: Save me the Roberto Clemente. He's taking me to Florida.

Dunn unfolded the bottom part of the sheet, exposing the contents. Seven baseball cards in plastic sleeves stared up at him. On the top a 1953 Bowman *Willie Mays.* The price stickers had been peeled off. Dunn gave a low whistle.

"I don't understand," Sasha began.

"I think I do," Dunn said slowly. He was quiet for a few minutes, piecing it together. "Moira spoke to you of escape. I don't think the gun was meant to be her escape. I think these were. Her ticket out." He paused. "Her wings. She was repaying you and trying for a new start for herself."

Sasha looked perplexed. "What on earth are they?"

Dunn answered: "To you and me, they look like something out of a Cracker Jack box. But if these are from the set I think they are, they could be worth a couple of thousand apiece. Not exactly retirement money, but enough to settle some debts. Or break with the past, if that's your inclination."

Sasha was shaking her head. "Sure doesn't sound like she was planning suicide."

Dunn agreed. "Thing is, we don't know when she mailed this. Might have been Friday after the last pickup. A lot can change in a few hours. Including moods." He remembered the videotape. This could be what Moira bought the stamp for at midnight.

"Where did she get them?" Sasha asked, studying the cards.

Dunn said: "I believe now she got these from Chris or his buddies. There's a good possibility they were involved in the break-in at the Sports King. These musta been part of the take." He rubbed the back of his head. "It's not typical of these guys to spread stolen property around among friends. Moira probably helped herself to them. Once they discovered the cards were gone they would've taken this place apart."

"Why didn't she just bring them over . . . Oh, right, she doesn't have a car. Anymore. It was totaled in her accident."

"Plus, they're out of everyone's reach for a few days until the heat's off," he added. *She had a better idea . . .*

Sasha shuddered. "Would they have killed her over those cards?"

Dunn looked at her. "Might have. Over the cards, and more importantly, over the betrayal and the fear she'd turn them in. If she could steal from them, she was capable of worse."

Moira's sister digested this for a moment. Then looked around. "It doesn't look like they did much searching, does it? If they killed her because they knew, and we know they didn't find the cards, why didn't they look for them?"

Dunn was still working it out. He started to walk around the small room. Finally: "Sasha, if you confronted someone who stole something from you, what would you do first?"

"Demand that they tell me where it was, I suppose. But what if they didn't want to tell me? How could I make them?"

"What if you had a gun? Or they did, and you got ahold of it?"

"Threaten them?"

"And when would you be most likely to carry out that threat?" he asked, staring out the window at the back of the Store 24.

Sasha answered: "When they told . . . when she told them where it was. Where it was going."

Dunn turned back to her. "I think you should stay with your father for a few days."

The girl nodded. "Post office kind of messed up her plans."

The detective folded everything carefully back together and shoved them into the envelope. Moira's Great Escape. "Post office and someone else. Your sister flew too close to the sun, Sasha."

Back in the office, Dunn laid the cards out on his desk and called Mr. Lazarus. They were indeed all from the Sports King break. He could hear Lazarus crying on the other end. Dunn was apparently slated for canonization. After Dunn hung up, Myles came over and studied the faces on the cards. America's heroes.

Softball was Myles's game. Half the Salem PD golfed, the other half played softball. The previous summer a po-lice officer vacationing from Oslo had stopped by the sta-tion to trade patches, stories, and go for a ride in a cruiser. The following Sunday morning, Orm the Red, they called him, was invited to join Salem's finest wage battle against the Beverly PD on the softball field down at the Willows. The Norwegian had never played softball, but once he was shown how to hold a bat, he could hit like a motherfucker and run like a sonofabitch. Twenty-five years of skiing to school and work every day had given Orm the power to bestow upon the Salem police their long-awaited and well-deserved place in history.

Orm had a chest and pair of arms that could stop a runaway freight train, and caught two flies in the first inning. Salem got in a bit of trouble, though, when Orm figured he was supposed to tag Beverly's runner with the ball, and nearly knocked him out cold in the process.

When Orm the Red was up to bat the first time, he swung at what would have been the ball to walk him, hit a grounder, and made first base with considerable verbal direction from his teammates. Salem's next man up struck out. The following batter connected with the ball and headed toward first base. Orm turned around and ran back to home plate, nearly colliding with the batter and so confusing Beverly's catcher that the guy nearly shot the Norseman. The Red crossed the plate cheering and yelling like a madman, hands held high. Pandemonium broke out. Talk about stealing home.

In the end, Salem won. Two of Beverly's players sustained minor injuries. After the game, Orm outdrank both municipalities and got his picture taken sitting in the twenty-one car.

"So Moira was cutting herself in, huh? Trying to steal home," said Myles. "Got tagged out in a squeeze play, Gabe. Suicide squeeze, they call it," he added with a smile.

Chapter 26

Night Moves

Dunn threw his jacket back on and left the office in search of an all-night stationery store. Jake Myles took the red car and headed in the opposite direction in search of some dinner. On his way, the red car was cut off in Riley Plaza by two kids on a Kawasaki with no headlight. Myles punched on the grill lights and hit the siren once. The kids pulled over, disconcerted by the unmarked car and its angry occupant flashing his badge and waving a light in their faces.

Myles leaned out the window and barked: "Lemme see your license."

The driver looked about sixteen. "I . . . I left it at home."

"Got any ID?"

"No, sir."

"Permit? Y-card?"

"No, sir."

"*Library* card?"

"No, sir."

Myles swung the light to the passenger. "Where the fuck's his helmet?"

"I don't have one . . ." the rider said in a small voice. He also had no ID. Probably the labels had been ripped out of their clothes.

"What happened to your headlight?" Myles demanded.

They chorused earnestly: "It just went out—on Highland, just now."

"All right, who are you?" he said to the driver.

The kid looked uncertain as to whether he was being addressed. After looking around, he answered, "Matthew."

"Matthew? Matthew who?"

"Pelletier," sounding like a guess.

"Who are you?" Myles yelled, illuminating the other perky countenance.

"Jeff."

"Jeff who?" with exaggerated patience.

"Lynch."

Myles loved kids. They never figure it out. There could be eight kids on the bike. He could do this seven times. And still the eighth would answer, *Jerry. Jerry who?* like a knock-knock joke.

"Where are you going in such a hurry?" Myles ground on.

"Beverly," barely audibly.

"Beverly? What's in Beverly?"

"A girl . . ."

After badgering them a while about their missing equipment and brain cell, Myles told them to get lost.

Beverly. A little after eight P.M. Judd slid his burly carcass behind the wheel of his Mustang and slammed the car door. *Need a plan, man. Gotta have a plan.* He switched on the ignition. Five minutes later, he rolled up quietly in front of Adele's place. Then he coasted a half block farther and turned around. Her lights were off, her car nowhere in sight. Judd decided to wait. He lit a cigarette, flipped on the radio, and rubbed his tattoo. The car smelled of Jergens hand lotion.

Chapter 27

Waiting for You

Adele gave the officer behind the desk a pleading look. She leaned toward the small hole in the plexiglass barrier. "Could you try again?"

"No one's there, ma'am. They're in and out. They don't check in with us. Just slip out the back door." Nevertheless, the man buzzed the CID's extension once more. Then he replaced the receiver. "Is it an emergency?"

"I . . . guess not. I wanted to tell him something. About the Moira Doheny case."

"I can take a message."

"Maybe I'll wait. He's coming back?"

The officer looked at the clock. Quarter to nine. "Should be."

The lobby was about four by eight feet and had no chairs. Entirely enclosed in glass and cheap paneling, it felt like a rather roomy phone booth. Adele stood for ten minutes reading some dedication plaque to a cop killed in World War II. Hurtgan Forest, Strass, Germany, the man of inspirational character drew his last breath. She wondered what it would be like to die in a place called Hurtgan Forest. You'd sit down and lean against some big oak tree, finding shelter from a light snow, clutching your side where the life ebbed slowly away. The rough bark at your back would comfort and enfold you. How could you have war in a forest? But dying in a forest. That was cool.

No other reading material to write home about. After a while she grew tired. "I'll wait in the car," she said through the hole in the plexiglass. No one looked up.

The Black Crowes cut was over. It was almost nine P.M. In the dark of the car, Judd surfed up and down the radio dial looking for something tolerable. *Shoulda done this last night . . .*

Judd considered the possibility for a moment that it was too late. The police might already have reached Adele, and she might not take long to put two and two together. She had been the only one he had told when he left to get the beer that night.

Suppose Adele decided to protect him? After all, what was in it for her, always the crucial question with Adele. The accident happened nine months ago. Moira was now dead, no longer suffering from her injuries. And it *had* been an accident. Judd was hurt himself, bruises up and down both arms and legs. Only he got no sympathy. Couldn't tell anyone. Couldn't risk the DWI, being out on parole. But the worst would have been Chris. The kid would have killed him soon as he was released. For being with Moira. And then for what happened. Moira was never the same. Fucking miracle she lost her memory.

Would she keep quiet? Judd found a tolerable Metallica song, cranked it up, and began to beat on imaginary drums. He laughed. Adele? *No fucking way.*

Dunn slid into a CID space in front of the station. Behind him a car honked. Across the intersection, rolling down her car window, was Adele Prada. Dunn stepped out of the Crown Vic, crossed the street, and leaned in.

"Hi," she said.

"Hi," responded the detective. "What are you doing here?"

"No place to wait inside."

"They tell us when we get the new station you'll have a place to sit."

She laughed, nervously but relieved now that he was here. "I can't wait that long. I just wanted to tell you something. About the night of the accident?"

"Yeah?" said Dunn with interest. "You want to come inside? I'll give you a chair."

"No, that's OK. I don't have that much to tell. Just that I'm pretty sure it was Judd Grimes who drove Moira that night. When you told me there was someone with her . . . that's who it had to be." Adele had never liked Judd. But now as her allegiance was shifting more and more toward Chris, her vengeance toward Judd was growing. Judd had turned Chris in. Judd had hurt Moira, Judd could hurt Chris tonight. "It came to me after you hung up. The party. In fact, the party was probably 'cause it was Moira's birthday. I hadn't even thought about it at the time. I never put the two of them together. But Judd was going out for beer, and probably borrowed Moira's car. Only she might not have trusted him with it alone, or else he lured her somehow. Which was like him. But that kind of party, you don't pay much attention when people leave and don't come back. When we heard about the accident, everyone was saying she was alone. So it never occurred to me to think about Judd. Then it connected. Kernwood goes to Beverly. Judd always kept spare cases around at his place, for Sundays especially."

"Saves a trip to New Hampshire," said Dunn.

"No, saves breaking into a liquor store in Salem. Anyway, Judd would never come forward about it. I think he was on probation last spring, or parole or something. Probably thought he'd get in trouble if anyone knew."

"He might have, yes. If he was at fault."

"He had a lot to drink."

"That'll do it," said Dunn. "Thanks, Adele. This helps."

She smiled. He had nice eyes. She started up the engine. Giving him Judd was a pleasure. Then, remembering the reason for her urgency, she held out her hand to stop him. "Wait. Chris knows. He went out looking for Judd tonight. Sergeant, he was ripped. I'm worried he might get hurt."

"Judd, or Chris?"

"Chris. I don't give a shit about Judd," she answered.

"Adele, you be careful," Dunn said. He watched while she pulled out and disappeared down Front Street.

When Dunn went upstairs Trinidad was occupied with visitors: the muffs, the incompetent bad boys, were back, looking like terrified children in a doctor's waiting room. Both were from Gloucester. Both were out of their element, wrong town, wrong shopping list. Wrong time warp.

"Still nothing?" Dunn asked Trinidad, who was reading a copy of *True Detective* while one of the men made a phone call.

Trinidad shook his head sadly. He turned the page and read aloud the ad for Swedish girls. "It says to call Britt."

Dunn was restless. He reached for the phone and called Samuel MacKenzie, the state ballistician, at home.

"Sam? Gabe Dunn. Sorry to bother you. The Doheny case? I think I've got a homicide. I know you won't do your tests for a while, I was just wondering if you had confirmed the caliber or anything."

"The bullets? Definitely a thirty-eight," MacKenzie responded. "What are you looking for, Gabe?"

"I don't know. I want to be sure that was the gun that killed Moira Doheny. The chemist ought to be able to find traces of her blood on the gun, given the range. I know I'm asking for a lot, but if I had a strong suspect in the next twenty-four hours or so, we might still be able to raise blood traces on his hands, too." Occult blood, invisible to the eye, was chemically detectable on skin for three or four days, with luck. Dunn had a suspect a few cases back who shaved and bleached his arms prior to the test. They still raised a couple spots of blood on his forearm.

"You got anyone in mind? They might voluntarily submit . . ." MacKenzie offered.

"A couple in mind, but there's a possibility I'll have narrowed it down tomorrow afternoon. I wanted a little more to back it up with in case he or she doesn't agree to be tested."

MacKenzie sighed. "I don't know about getting you test shots in time. I'll at least check the lands and grooves on the bullets for you. I can probably nail the manufacturer of the gun. What's tomorrow . . . Tuesday? Call me late tomorrow morning."

"Sam? At the post, what did you say was in her head, a practice load?"

"Looked like it, yeah."

"Let's make sure we got aluminum shells in the gun."

As soon as he hung up, the phone rang. Dunn lifted the still warm receiver. It was Jake Myles calling from the red car.

"Gabe? I'm on Ward Street talking to young Carlos. Our friend the shortstop."

Dunn switched ears. "Yeah?"

"Says he was at this girl's place this afternoon. She had a visitor, some sort of business transaction he didn't want to go into and we couldn't possibly guess at."

"She's probably the Avon lady."

Myles continued: "That's right. Anyway, this visitor, he's waiting around for her runner to get there, I guess she was out of bath-oil beads. He's all fidgety and talkative and stuff. You know how guys get."

"Yeah. Alligator skin. Hate it when that happens," Dunn said sympathetically.

"He mentions some girls he knew, you know guys do that, too, sometimes. Anyway, he mentions the name 'Moira.' "

"Does he?" Dunn straightened up with interest.

"He also mentions 'Adele.' Now 'Moira,' she is no happy individual, according to Carlos. She has come to some unfortune, from the sound of it."

"He was pretty good at bat, wasn't he?" Dunn asked.

"Carlos? I thought we walked him. But you're the one with the memory. Anyway, then this guy . . ."

"Whose name is?"

" 'John.' "

"Oh, right. We know 'John,' " Dunn said.

"This guy 'John' tells Carlos and this lady that Adele, well, she's in for some unfortune, too."

Dunn stood up. "What kind of unfortune, did he say, Jake?"

"If only we knew what 'unfortune' meant, we could probably take precautionary . . ."

"Jake, what else did he say?" Dunn had unbuckled his belt and was threading his holster back on.

"The guy asked Carlos if he knew where he could get a gun."

"Did he?"

Myles answered: "Carlos didn't know that word, 'gun.' And I guess guns weren't in Avon's fall line . . ."

Dunn reached for his jacket. "Meet me at Adele's, Jake. Like right now."

"You know who this guy is?"

"Yeah. I know who he is." Dunn hung up and radioed the twenty-six car.

Chapter 28

Knockin' on Heaven's Door

Judd could see headlights coming down Upham Street. As they slowed, he knew it was Adele's Baretta. She pulled into a spot close to the front of her house. Judd heard the car door slam and watched her mount the front steps, fumbling for her keys. She would not have noticed him, sandwiched between two cars a hundred feet farther down. No one would have noticed him.

He waited until she was inside. The back door was his best bet. Surprise her, in case she wasn't feeling sociable.

Judd reached inside his jacket pocket and felt for the fishing knife. All eight inches were there, not including the handle. With one hand he switched off the radio and removed his keys. Simultaneously, his left arm swung wide the car door.

In the instant the music stopped, Judd Grimes heard the roar of the motorcycle, but he heard it too late. Two kids, returning home from a failed rendezvous in Beverly, watching out only for red Crown Victorias, hadn't observed Judd's Mustang because Judd was good at parking unobservedly. Judd hadn't noticed the motorcycle because its headlight was burned out.

When the bike and door connected, they were cushioned by Judd's left forearm, his business arm, newly tattooed. The arm snapped, the door underwent an adjustment, the Kawasaki spilled. The kid in back had no helmet and slumped unconscious against the opposite curb.

Officer Frank Mallory, twenty-six car, father of two, caught the call. When he arrived Mallory found himself in the middle of an altercation following a vehicle accident. One of the injured was clutching a broken arm and kicking someone or something in the street. The man appeared to be half crazed with anger, an anger that Mallory seriously underestimated. Metal flashed as a knife was produced, reflecting the solitary streetlight, stunning and stinging the policeman before he knew what had happened. Warmth from out of nowhere began to spread across his shirt. Mallory reached for the radio on his belt and called for assistance. It seemed an understatement.

Nothing makes your blood run colder than hearing a cop's voice on the radio calling for help. Suddenly there are no choices, no decisions to make. You drop your coffee and punch the lights and sirens. You move.

Dunn was already on the way. He had just turned onto North Street when he heard the call. Covering the remaining blocks in just under a minute and a half, he turned onto Upham Street to find himself third to respond, behind twenty-seven and twenty-two cars. Dunn braked hard and came to a stop in what could have been a movie set, blazing with lights and boiling with churning figures. As he jumped out, twenty-three car slid in behind him, then twenty-one, then twenty-five, then thirty-six. In the middle of the road, illuminated by the street light, was Mallory's hat.

In front of the twenty-six car was Mallory, lying still and clutching the sleeve of one of the two beat men from the point.

As Dunn approached, two ambulances rounded the corner and plowed onto the set. Behind them were the twenty-eight car and Myles.

A man laid out. Only this was one of their own.

We don't say, that could have been me. We say, that's me.

Chapter 29

Down and Out

Dunn and Myles rode together to Judd's address in Beverly, followed by a couple of backups. No sign of a Mustang with a tormented door on Federal Street. The detectives waited for one of the patrolmen to move into position behind the apartment building, then went into the lobby and buzzed a few bells on the first floor until a man in a bathrobe came out and let them in.

On the third floor, guns drawn, they flattened out on each side of Judd's door. A New England Telephone ad sang out from across the hall. Myles rapped loudly and yelled, "Police." After a few moments of silence, the owner of the TV peered out at them, then withdrew. There was no response from Judd's apartment. Myles looked at Dunn. "We goin' in?" he asked.

Dunn shook his head. "Hold it. I don't think he's here." He walked down to the window at the end of the hall and looked out. Officer Szymanski stood out in front listening to his radio. Across the street St. Mary, Star of the Sea, was wrapped in shadow, save for her illuminated sign, like a beacon in the night. BEANO. Seven P.M.

A discontinuity on the school steps caught Dunn's attention. "Wait here," he said to Myles, and went back downstairs. After a word with Szymanski outside, Dunn walked across to the school. He approached the front steps slowly.

Chris Alexei crouched at the top, enshrouded in dark and leaning against a pillar. He barely moved as the detective came over beside him. "He ain't in there," Chris said.

"Where is he?" asked Dunn.

Chris shrugged. "When he comes home, he'll fucking regret it."

"Mind if I wait with you?" Dunn asked, sitting down.

The boy pulled out a pack of cigarettes.

The detective leaned forward with his arms on his knees. "He may be running right now. We think he's hurt. We know he's dangerous."

Chris kept his eyes on the apartment building. "Sounds like Judd. Just another shitty day in paradise." He was quiet for a while. Then he spoke again: "Judd's good at running. And hurting." A long pause. "I always thought something was going on with him and Moira, you know. When I got out last year, he was acting *strange*. I mean, he had tried to hang around her before. Judd had a real thing for her. But the kid's such a slug. I didn't worry much, until I came back and Moira was all fucked up, not remembering anything, wanting to be by herself, and there's Judd acting like he owed you money. Kind of like guilty, only the kid doesn't know how to feel guilty."

Dunn didn't say anything. His radio crackled softly. He pressed the button. "Yes, Jake?"

"Uh, thirty-three, what am I doing?" Myles asked.

"You're waiting," Dunn answered. Then he radioed Szymanski to go upstairs and keep him company. He waited for Chris to continue.

"Tonight Adele told me Judd was the cause of Moira's accident. That's what he was being strange about. She went through all that, she went through fucking hell and she never knew what for." He put his head down. "I even accused her of messing around. He knew I was suspecting her. And that it hurt her. And he never came forward. About any of it."

They watched a few cars go by. The boy finally lit his cigarette and extended the pack to Dunn. The detective shook his head with regret. Chris watched the lighter's flame for a while, his dark-framed face illuminated like a baroque painting. Dunn thought about Moira and all the misplaced blame and doubt she must have endured. Injury without explanation. Suffering without understanding. Pain without memory.

"What's 'Star of the Sea' mean?" Chris asked, blowing softly to bend the flame.

"Beats me," said Dunn. He found himself inhaling Chris's smoke and fought off the enjoyment. "Is that one of Judd's lighters?"

Chris grunted in affirmation. "His calling cards." He extinguished the light. For a few seconds Dunn could no longer see him. The streetlight illuminated only the tips of their shoes. "Were you scared of the dark when you were a kid?" Chris asked.

Dunn smiled. "Yeah, I was, actually. I used to ask them to leave the light on when I slept. But I shared a room with two big brothers who wouldn't hear of it."

"The light bothered them?"

"Well, I thought when I explained about the monsters they'd agree. Incredibly, I couldn't get through to them. So I used to sleep sitting up in my bed with a laundry basket over my head for protection."

"Still do?" asked Chris.

"Not very often," said Dunn.

"I was the opposite," Chris said. "I always preferred the dark. I think from the time I could walk." He sucked on his teeth. "Judd know you guys are after him?"

"I would think so."

Chris pulled on his cigarette. The tip glowed brightly.

"He may not come back here, then. Even a halfwit like him could figure that much out."

Dunn nodded and waited.

Chris continued: "There's a place in Lynn he'll probably go. A friend of his. Especially if he needs help. It's on Sutton Avenue. Number 253. Across from the Shell station."

Dunn relayed this information to Myles. "Leave Szymanski here, in case he does show up. You can come on down." He put the radio down and said to Chris: "We need to talk, you and I. About some cards. Why don't you leave Judd to us for now."

Chris dropped his cigarette on the step and crushed it with his toe. "Like I have a choice?" He stood up heavily. "Sounds like a brand of tuna fish, don't it?"

"What's that?" asked Dunn.

"Saint Mary, Star of the Sea. You think I'll get out tomorrow in time for the funeral?" Chris knew he would be charged before the night was over.

"We'll do what we can," replied Dunn, and walked him to the car.

Chapter 30

Stakeouts

On his way to the station Tuesday morning, Dunn stopped at the hospital to check on Frank Mallory, then to the Salem post office, where he arranged a favor with the supervisor. The detective handed over a red envelope to be given to Sasha Doheny's carrier, an envelope for which he paid postage. That was part of the deal.

Dunn entered the detectives' office and nodded to the assorted members of the day shift. "Jake in?" he asked.

"Went for coffee," the juvenile officer responded. Since Mazurka worked with kids, he was given the smallest desk. Almost a pretend desk, tucked at the end of one of the rows like an errant child's. A toy desk, whose drawers were crammed with toy guns which looked frighteningly real, and toy knives which were no joke.

Dunn threw his jacket onto the filing cabinet. There was a note on his desk. A phone message from Samuel Mac-Kenzie. It read:

> Tell Gabe: Federal (brass) and aluminum
> casings in cylinder. Federal fired last.
> Lands and grooves consistent with a Charter
> Arms Bulldog. Confirmed bullet in deceased
> practice round. Bullet in wall jacketed

hollow-point. Probably the Federal. Can
send to FBI to confirm. Let me know.

—Sam

Dunn grinned. Moira died with a practice bullet in her
brain. The kind that come in disposable aluminum shells.
The Federal bullet, fired second, had to have been fired by
someone other than Moira. He dialed Gloria Mei and told
her she could change the "pending."

Twenty minutes later Myles returned to loud complaints
over his timeliness. He glanced over at Dunn. "Lynn police
are still watching that Sutton Avenue location. No sign of
him either place yet."

"He'll show," said Dunn.

"How's Frankie?" Myles asked, unpacking the bag of
Charlie Novembers, code for cream-no-sugars. He passed
one to Braedon, one to Mazurka, set one aside for the
chief, and pried open the fourth. Light-brown liquid had
seeped through the bag. Myles began his usual morning
diversionary rescue and cleanup operation, salvaging the
most critical components of the layer on his desk from the
ensuing puddle.

"Still in intensive care. They're hoping to upgrade him
later today," Dunn answered.

"How about my kids? Mutt and Jeff?" asked Myles, who
regretted having let the bikers go.

"The one without the helmet will recover, but he'll be in
for a while. The driver warded Grimes off somehow, then
bolted. Probably saved his life. He's just scratched up a
bit."

"Peabody called," said Myles. "They picked up a guy
early this morning who may be one of our thieves. I left a
note for Sheila. Chris on his way to court?"

Dunn looked at the clock. "Soon. I'll go check on him.

Take him some coffee." To work a deal, Chris had helped them close eleven cases during the night. Sheila Tobias had come in, they divvied up the paperwork, shared a pizza with their prisoner, and put together a package for the DA. A low bail, concurrent sentences, and less of his past to bite him unexpectedly when he came up for parole, provided Chris's motivation; closing cases was the cops'. Dunn and Tobias had kept Chris talking. Myles had kept the copier rolling. Teamwork all around. By the time they had taken Chris downstairs, he had been too tired to care about the rats.

Myles threw a soggy pile of napkins into the wastebasket. "Solved the Doheny case yet?"

Dunn answered: "No, but we have an appointment this afternoon. Could help."

"With who?" asked Myles.

"Moira's killer. We'll leave at noon. Be here. I don't want to be late."

"Moira's killer? You're shittin' me."

"He's expecting a small package at Sasha's. We need to be sure he gets it."

"Gets what?" Myles wasn't getting it.

"His package. Just one of the many services we provide." Dunn reached for the chief's unclaimed coffee. "Anyone drinking this?" he asked.

Chris Alexei was lying on his back staring at the ceiling. The bunks in the holding cells were clearly not meant for sleeping. He sat up and looked at Dunn expectantly.

"Be about a half hour," said the detective. He unlocked the cell door and handed the boy the coffee.

"I couldn't have a cigarette, could I?" Chris asked. "I've got some in my jacket."

Dunn went out into the booking office and located Chris's laundry basket. Crouching down, he reached under the boy's sneakers for the jacket and felt through the pockets. He pulled out the pack and lighter. As he started to drop the coat back in, Dunn's gaze fell on Chris's left shoe, now turned upside down. The detective knelt down for a closer look. On the bottom and edge of the instep were traces of brown stain, thicker than water, thinner than mud. Much of whatever the boy had stepped into had been worn off, or left behind in slushy patches over the last few days. But Dunn was certain enough remained, crammed up in the treads, to be typed. He no longer had to blame his own department for screwing up the crime scene. Not this crime scene, at least.

Dunn walked quietly back to the cell, carrying the shoe and cigarettes.

"I need you to explain one more thing, son," he said. Holding up the sneaker, he ventured: "I need you to explain Moira's blood on your shoe." The detective located a fresh Miranda card, Mirandized the boy and repeated his question. Chris didn't answer.

"When you told us about all the B and E's, you must have overlooked the homicide." continued Dunn. He took a seat on the bunk opposite Chris.

"Why would I kill Moira?"

Dunn leaned back and waited.

Chris rested the coffee on the floor. He lit his cigarette, handed the lighter back to Dunn, then folded his hands. Finally, he met Dunn's eyes. "Saturday morning. We went over to move the cards. They had been down in the shelter, where you found the sticker."

" 'We?' " asked Dunn. "Thought you said you were alone on those jobs."

"You believed that?"

"No. Who was with you, Chris?"

Chris looked at his hands. "I can't tell you. You know

that. I'll get the cards back. But I have a reputation to protect."

"Go on," said Dunn. "We'll get back to that."

Chris continued: "I went inside to see Moira. Let her know I was out of jail."

"You have a key?"

Chris smiled faintly. "Key? What's that? I pass through walls, remember?" The expression dropped off his face. "It didn't take long to find her. Laying in the living room. Looked like she shot herself. I got the hell out of there. Told . . . my friend. We took the cards and split." He looked at the shoe, resting next to the policeman on the bunk. "I guess I stepped in the blood when I went up to her."

"You touch her?"

"I touched her face. Brushed it, kind of. That's all I touched. Not the gun, not anything."

"And it never occurred to you to tell anyone?" asked Dunn.

"Of course it occurred to me. But it didn't look like a murderer was getting away, I mean, she killed herself, it looked like." He added in a low voice: "And I was worried, of course."

Dunn stood up. "Can I keep the shoes?" He had sufficient probable cause to take them, but consent was much easier.

"What am I gonna wear to my arraignment?"

"I'll get you a real nice pair," said Dunn.

Chapter 31

The Pickup

The mailbox was black metal with a swivel lid and a horse and carriage in relief on the front, painted white and giving it a kind of classy Beverly Farms attitude. Dunn and Myles sat in an impounded Thunderbird around the corner on Milk Street. They had a good view of Sasha's house and looked only as suspicious as they usually did, two guys sitting in a car for an hour on a gusty Tuesday afternoon. Myles cranked up the radio.

"Any bets?" he asked Dunn.

Dunn smiled but didn't speak.

At the far end of Pickman the first player appeared, leather pouch slung over her gray-jacketed shoulder. The letter carrier worked her way slowly up the walk of Number 8 Pickman, and dropped a bundle of letters through the slot in the door.

It occurred to Dunn that the killer probably would be staking out the house, too. No point in leaving twelve thousand dollars worth of baseball cards unattended in an outside mailbox for too long. He twisted around in his seat and looked down Milk Street, searching for other occupied cars.

The postman had made her way to Number 10. This time she struggled a moment to squeeze a couple of maga-

180

zines into an under-sized box. A breeze whipped short brown hair into her face.

Dunn's leg was falling asleep. He hoped the killer was in fact watching. He hoped this would be quick.

They should have looked for other cars when they came up Webb Street. Anyone else waiting for the mail wouldn't have been able to pinpoint the delivery time. They probably would have been there much earlier. Probably watched the Thunderbird set up. Dunn sighed. Never assume you're dealing with an amateur. Staking out a drug deal you come well before the appointed time, because you can be sure the seller will. To look for the cops and to hide his stash. With chagrin, he realized his mistake. The purpose hadn't been to get to Pickman before the mailman. The purpose was to get there before the killer.

Myles turned down the music. "So who upgraded this to a homicide?"

"Samuel MacKenzie," answered Dunn.

Number 24's box was perched on a low fence in front, the kind of round-topped box with the door in one end. This one was angled back slightly. Dunn wondered if it filled up with rain.

And then she walked up to the door of 28, lifted the black metal top, and dropped in three envelopes. The middle one extended out and was red. Dunn straightened up slowly.

The postman continued down the street. The remaining stops passed in slow motion. At Number 36, she stopped to have a few words with a man who stuck his head out the door. No one else had yet appeared on the street. Dunn pressed his forehead against the rim of the steering wheel. Maybe the killer was waiting for Ms. Postman to get lost. Maybe he was waiting for the very conspicuous Thunderbird to get lost. Maybe this whole theory sucked. *What screws up your landings is the wind* . . . He closed his eyes and felt the car rock slightly with each gust. *If it's blowing you to the left, give it left rudder—right aileron . . .* Or was it right rudder—left aileron? The hardest part of flying was knowing the difference between where you're pointing and where you're going. You could point her straight down the runway and still end up landing somewhere out in east bumfuck. Dunn looked back up and scanned the street. For ten more minutes he choked on Myles's cigarette smoke and listened to the man whine.

And then at the far end of the street, player Number 2 came into view, rounding the same corner the postman had started from. Dunn felt the back of his neck come to attention. He lifted the field glasses to his eyes and waited for the man, if it was a man, to come nearer. At Number 28, he turned and strode up the walk. Pulling out a red envelope, he lifted the top of the mailbox and busied himself with the insertion. When the hand withdrew, Dunn saw an unmistakable flash of red. The man turned and came back down the walk. The breeze wrapped hair around him like a muffler. But then the gust died, the hair fell, and a face appeared. Dunn lowered the glasses and handed them to Myles. *Straight down the runway.*

Eugene Sollors turned right and headed back the way he had come.

Detective Sheila Tobias knocked on the door of the Peabody CID and was invited in. A detective from Marblehead was pawing through a pile of stolen property on a conference table. One of the Peabody detectives was writing a pile of reports, the other was interrogating their suspect, white jeans, heavy flannel shirt over a T-shirt that said Tufts, and stocking feet. The suspect was wandering around the office. Tobias joined the line at the table. "That's mine," said Marblehead, picking up a small safe with the lid pried open. "Show me everything that was inside," he asked the kid.

The kid shrugged. He picked up one of several watches, and pointed to a stack of First Day covers, with nice stamps and neat postmarks. "I don't remember. These? Can I eat this?" He touched a stick of Big Red chewing gum. The entire contents of his car were laid out on the table. Some of it was legitimately his.

Peabody was trying to get him to remember where a couple of car radios had come from. The kid had admitted to three separate break-ins. None had included car radios. "You said you gave us everything," barked the detective. "How do you explain these?"

The kid walked around to the other side of the table and reached for a bottle of Polo Men's cologne. "Someone gave 'em to me." He squirted both sides of his neck and replaced it in the pile. Tobias gagged. The men swore.

"What are all these hats for? You got a dozen fucking hats," laughed Marblehead, indicating a multicolored stack of baseball caps, still with price tags.

"Those're from the Li'l Peach," the kid offered. The job in Swampscott two nights ago.

"But why?" Marblehead was really curious.

"Fashion," mumbled the kid, still looking through the pile for his own stuff.

Tobias looked through her file and compared her list with the items on display. Nothing identifiable matched. She felt like the low bidder at an auction. Marblehead—it was Marblehead's day. The detective reached forward again, snagging a car phone and reeling it in. From his own list, he located a serial number that matched. "This one's mine, too. This was from last night! A house on West Shore Drive—car phone was in the house. Wasn't it?" he asked the boy.

The kid found another stick of gum and continued eat-ing his way through the evidence. The Polo had filled the room, growing stronger as they talked.

The Peabody detective started yelling. "Marblehead last night, too? You said you told us everything."

"Well, now I have," said the kid in a faint voice.

"When you told us everything before, you, like, fucking *forgot* about the job you did last night?"

The boy didn't answer or look up.

"Huh? You forgot about it?"

"No."

"What?" the detective leaned over him.

"I didn't realize about it." Eloquence under pressure.

Tobias found some coins from a collection she thought might be hers. After a bit of discussion they convinced the boy to remember a house break in Salem two weeks ago. One case cleared, but no endorsed checks, no top shelf liquor, and the cash on the table was unidentifiable. A few gloves, but new and paired.

Peabody brought the party to a close. The detective stood up. "All right, kid. Show us what's yours."

Tobias thanked them for inviting her. Everything had been photographed; she signed a receipt, took her coins, and left.

It was a touching gesture from an old friend of the dearly departed. Tucked inside a red envelope addressed to Sasha was a flowery sympathy card, gilt letters, biblical passage, rosaries, birds, lilies, sentimental doodads, rays of sunlight through arched stained glass, signed Eugene Sollors, his real name, no alias. Solar power. Mr. Sunshine.

Hand delivered for the personal touch, and because you can't trust the post office at a time like this. But mainly it offered Sollors a convenient excuse to get into Sasha's mailbox, and switching red envelopes is less obtrusive than merely stealing one. Sasha was the winner in this trade.

Sollors wound up with a piece of the *Salem Evening News* and a few empty plastic sleeves. Sasha wound up with this fine sympathy card.

Myles reread the card, glanced at the envelope, then said to Dunn: "This guy a classmate of yours? He spells worse than you."

Dunn looked at him. "No one's worse than me."

Myles showed him the envelope. D-O-H-E-N-N-Y. "Now, I've known some Dohenys in my time. They're always being misspelled. But the usual way is D-O-N-N-E-H-Y. That's the acceptable misspelling."

Dunn studied the envelope. Name looked fine to him. "Yeah, right," he said.

"Anyway, the sympathy card was a nice touch, don't you think? Can we pop him now?"

"Not just yet, Jake. I need a bigger crime than a spelling mistake."

"Tampering with the mail?" Myles offered.

"I was hoping for a bit more. Let's not screw the pitch. And remember, we sort of tampered first."

Back at his desk, the Hello line rang and Dunn picked it up. It was Warren. Rachel had finally gone to see a doctor. Her mysterious and overly dramatic internal turmoil was now partially explained: She was pregnant. "Way to go, Warren," Dunn remarked. Rachel always did love kids. This should cheer her up. But knowing his sister, further battles would be just around the corner. This motherless child found comfort in chaos.

Chapter 32

Like a Rock

Mel Isaksen steered her sputtering Corolla down Exit 38 and limped into the Texaco station God had placed at the bottom of the hill for her. She had worn a skirt today for a parent conference. A nice, polite skirt, to get her through a not very encouraging progress report on their son. She hated skirts. Problem solving is always harder in a skirt. Her Corolla had a problem. And it was raining. And this was only Tuesday. It was going to be a long week.

The attendant suggested, after a cursory look, that it might be the fuel pump. Whatever it might be, the garage had closed for the evening. She was going to have to leave the car overnight, or call for a tow to a more helpful location, if one could be found. Mel didn't hold out much hope. She pulled the car key off the key ring and asked to use the phone.

Dunn's voice immediately reassured her. Mel felt apologetic. She knew he was busy solving murders and worrying about his sister. Mel also wasn't sure whether the recent progression in her relationship with this man warranted this degree of imposition yet. Finally, she felt keenly disappointed at the helplessness of her situation. Goddamn fuel pump. Mel didn't mind poking around under the hood of her car. She could deal with a few basic problems, change a tire, jumpstart her battery, dry off wires, unstick a choke.

Getting her car running again was far more empowering than cooking gravy with no lumps, though each probably had its place in the overall scheme of things.

"My car died."

"Where are you?" he asked.

"Stoneham, I think." She got the address from the attendant.

Dunn offered to dig up one of the patrolmen who ran his own repair business after hours. Took pretty good care of half the department's personal vehicles. Mel declined.

"They'll fix it here tomorrow, and I can get a ride to school in the morning."

"All right, just sit tight. I'll be there in twenty minutes."

"Gabe, I'm sorry. This is so stupid. I don't know anything about fuel pumps, or I would have . . ."

"I don't know anything about fuel pumps, either. If it had happened to me, I would have called *you* for a ride. And you would have come and gotten me, right?"

"Of course."

"You don't owe me any apologies, Mel. You don't need to prove anything to me. I'll see you in twenty minutes."

Mel hung up and leaned against the booth. Why was it so easy to abdicate responsibility here? Why did it feel so good to be comforted? To be rescued? Why did she feel so needy? Why was this such a complicated transaction? Why hadn't she called her girlfriend, Olivia? Olivia lived in Danvers and could fetch her just as easily. Olivia wouldn't have minded, it wouldn't have been a big deal. Mel wouldn't be feeling particularly helpless, certainly not defensive.

She wanted Dunn to rescue her. Maybe she wanted him to demonstrate that he still remembered her the morning after, so to speak. That now they had slept together, he wasn't going to stop caring about her.

Did he care about her? How the hell did she know?

When he was with her, he was great. But too much time passed between calls, and too many dates got canceled. How could he love her and not be absolutely compelled to see her whenever possible?

Mel could be tough and independent. She had convinced a number of men that she had not needed them. That she could live without them. Mel wasn't sure she wanted to convince Dunn of that.

She looked at her watch. It was nearly five-thirty. Dunn would have a lot of traffic on 128. She opened the phone booth door and went back inside the station. Under the garish fluorescent light, she settled onto a rusty folding chair among a pyramid of 10W30 oil cans on display. Her pale-yellow hair took on a greenish tinge in the shop window. Mel had a pretty good figure, though. Maybe she would help Texaco sell some oil.

The gray unmarked cruiser pulled up in front of the window. Dunn had in fact taken only twenty minutes. Mel decided not to ask what kind of stunts he had pulled to get by the rush-hour logjam. She got into the warm car, pushing her briefcase down into a pile of styrofoam cups. *Glad to see you're not a fussy little anal retentive neatness freak,* she managed not to say.

"How's your case coming?" she asked instead, and forcibly held back another lame apology. Somehow most of her opening conversation was being filtered out. She was uncomfortable, wondering if he was annoyed or pleased to see her. Also she thought she might be sitting on a nightstick.

"Good," he said. "I think I've got my suspect on the hook. Just have to figure out how to reel him in."

Mel nodded. Reeling in was the tough part. *You think you finally have someone on the hook, but it's too, too easy for them to just slip away, Gabe.* The schoolteacher had been watching previews for ten months. When was the Greatest Love Story of the Century finally going to begin?

"You looked very pretty perched in the window with all those cans," Dunn said. "I was tempted to ask for an oil change."

Cute, she thought. *Why don't you put your arm around me and ask me how I'm doing? Let the comforting begin . . .*

Dunn merged back onto Route 128 and picked out his lane. Then he turned to look at Mel. "How are you doing?" he said, slipping an arm around her shoulder.

"I'm OK," she said, making herself be strong again. "How's your sister?"

"She's pregnant."

Mel looked at Dunn. "Is she happy about it?"

"Rachel doesn't know how to be happy." He was silent for another mile. Mel began to feel bad about all her romance novel machinations. Women around Dunn were getting pregnant, dropping dead, and God knows what. Mel's problem was that she needed a ride home. The longing, the Sturm und Drang she had felt in the Texaco window had set the women's movement back thirty years.

Finally, Dunn spoke again. "I should never have let Claire leave the state. I should have fought for custody."

"Claire?" It took a moment for Mel to realize he was no longer talking about his sister's happiness. He was talking about his own. Mel's heart began to ache for him. So this was the baggage he was carrying around. This was the Great Detective's Angst. "Do you think you really could have won?" she asked him.

"No. But I wouldn't be punishing myself for the past five years for not trying. How could I have just let her go?"

"How often do you see her? Joy?" Mel was on a roll with parent conferences today.

"I drive out every few weeks, when I'm not grabbing overtime. It's about four hours each way. I had this dream when I started flying lessons that I could fly out every weekend and somehow stay in her life. It takes half as long by plane. Claire lives about three blocks from a little grass strip. I had it all worked out. Pretty crazy plan. Between alimony, child support, and making my fat flight instructor very rich, I'm no closer to her now than I was five years ago. There goes that particular sandcastle. Washing out to sea. She's getting a life of her own there. I'm what's known as a Disneyland Daddy."

"Maybe you should put your money into a good lawyer."

"I have no case, Mel. Claire's got family out there. Joy stays with her grandmother during the day. What can I offer her? Park her in the detective's office in front of a stolen TV all day? Give her my beeper number?"

"Kids can be amazingly flexible . . ."

"Who's gonna read to her at night? The only thing I can read out loud is a Miranda card."

Mel wanted to offer. She had her own little sand castle. She could quit her job. She could do gravy without lumps. Fuck the women's movement. "How about Rachel? Your sister could help out. Joy has plenty of family in Salem, too. She's starting school in a few months, Gabe. There's nothing shameful about day care in the meantime. Talk to a lawyer. Maybe you could at least work out shared custody. Or maybe you'll lose. But like you said, you'll know you tried." Sometimes giving comfort was just as comforting as getting it. Clearly, Dunn was the one needing rescuing today. Mel never realized he thought so little of himself as a father, and that it bothered him so much.

Dunn was listening. And thinking.

"And just as importantly," she continued, "Joy will know you tried."

Dunn pulled over into the breakdown lane and rolled to a stop. He watched the cars speed by for a few seconds. Then he pulled Mel toward him.

Chapter 33

Dyslexics Untie

When Dunn got back to the office Tuesday night, Billy Trinidad was alone. Dunn gave him a questioning shrug.

"The muffs?" Trinidad laughed. "I felt sorry for them. You never seen anyone try so hard to score. I swear, Gabe. I even took 'em down and parked them in front of the Lincoln Hotel. Xeroxed a twenty-dollar bill, told them to bring me a few fuckin' joints, for chrissake. Never seen that street dry up so fast. They stood there nearly an hour, trying not to look stupid. I finally reeled them in—I was bustin' a gut watching them. Just a couple of muffs, you know." He grinned. "Couple of mickey muffs. I'll talk to the DA anyway."

Dunn nodded his agreement. He hung up his leather jacket, put the radio battery in the recharger, then went over to Moira's typewriter. Reaching inside, he snapped off the ribbon cartridge and took it over to his desk. Myles came in wearing his uniform, on his way to a private detail, with some time to kill.

Dunn looked up. "Where you working?"

"Big Fred's. Did you get the message?"

"What message?" Dunn pawed through the slips on his desk.

"Lynn police called. They picked up Judd Grimes. At the Sutton Avenue address. Do you want to go get him?"

Dunn answered. "Could you ask the desk to send a cruiser?" He picked up the ribbon.

"How'd your boy's arraignment go this time?" Myles asked as he dialed downstairs.

"Adele Prada helped him make bail," Dunn answered as he studied the ribbon.

"They should give him his own parking place down at the courthouse—he's there every day," Myles continued after talking to the front desk.

The order of the letters was backward. Right up Dunn's alley. The ribbon was carbon, making it easy to read. Dunn thanked Moira silently for her wise investment. He then embarked on the laborious and challenging task of copying each letter onto a piece of paper. He set out in front of him the standard they had made, realizing with chagrin that they had broken a cardinal textbook rule and used the same ribbon for the test. Next to it he placed the suicide note, and next to that, Moira's note to her sister.

For a moment he considered asking Myles for help. But a strange, stubborn mixture of shame and pride stopped him. *Dyslexics Untie.* He switched on his desk lamp, unrolled about a foot of ribbon, and laid it out carefully before him. If only the letters themselves were backward, he could have used a mirror and the job would have been easier. By starting at the bottom of a sheet and writing the letters from right to left, his reproduction of the note would come out in the right order. He only had to figure out the spaces. Dunn pulled out a fresh sheet of paper and a pencil and began to hum.

Myles put his feet up and started twirling his hat on his finger. He looked over at Trinidad and said: "You know, Billy, I'm jealous. Yours looks so fine, I want to turn *my* desk around, too."

"Fuck yourself," replied Trinidad, who had begun to dismantle the phone-answering machine. They didn't call him Inspector Gadget for nothing.

"Gabe, OK if I turn my desk around?" Myles asked.

"What time's your job, Jake?" Dunn replied, without taking his eyes off the ribbon.

The first several inches consisted of their test typing; every keyboard row, shifted and unshifted. Finally he picked out:

arioM-evolhtiw

and thereafter, the body of the note. He unrolled another foot, and picked out the beginning of the note:

:nrecnocyamtimohwoT

followed immediately by:

arioM-evolhtiw

Dunn stopped humming. Then he remembered. As part of the test sample, they had typed the note in its entirety, to make the comparison easier. He resumed humming and threaded his way backward through what now was the real note.

"What are you singing, buddy?" Myles asked. "Sounds like the theme from *Rocky.*"

Dunn ignored him. *Untied we stand . . . Dived we fall.* No, *Divvied we fall.* He continued:

emevigrofnacllauoyepohI

Forgive, Moira, but not forget.

"Go for it!" Myles said from across the room.

Trinidad threw down his screwdriver. "This's a piece of

shit. I'm going downstairs later tonight and swap it for the one in Traffic."

Finally the "To whom it may concern:" reappeared. Dunn straightened up and wiped his palms off on his jeans. Now for the final act. He should in theory see the note to Sasha next.

But what appeared, frame by frame, letter by letter, was another copy of the suicide note.

Dunn swung his eyes back to their test page. Had they typed it twice? Reassured that they had not, he returned to the ribbon. A first draft. With some imperfection possibly. He worked his way backward through the note, faithfully copying each letter with his pencil.

When he was done, his version of the first draft read:

Towhomitmayconcern:Ihopeyouall
canforgivemeforwhatimu
stdo.Idontmeantohufxrtanyonebutthepainis
mortheaniIca
nstandThisistheolnyxxxnlywayout.Love,Moira
Dohenny

The author of this note was no professional typist. The final draft must have been done with painstaking care. To be perfect, the way Moira Doheny would have typed it. And the author had had a change of heart in the salutation at the end. Moira would have been less formal. She wouldn't have used her last name. For several minutes, Dunn stared at the letters, willing the squirrely bastards to stand in formation and hold still. Words lie. Especially lower case. *OK, Sollors. Final round. Ninth inning. Where's your signature?* And then he saw it. The oozing mass of letters froze for one instant. *Dohenny.*

"Jake, where's that sympathy card to Sasha?"

Divided we fall.

Chapter 34

Lady Sings the Blues

"Where's Billy?" Dunn asked the chief of detectives Wednesday morning.

"You mean Inspector *Gadget?*" Lieutenant Angeramo bellowed from the inner office. A good day was an Angeramo vacation day. "Three days, I gave him."

"What? Suspended? Carl, what the hell for? I'm wrapping up a murder investigation. I need him!" Dunn stared at him with disbelief.

"Last night, cloaked in darkness, young William attempted to switch the burned-out left headlight on the gray car for one from the twenty-six car."

Dunn's jaw dropped. This was getting weird. "You gave him three days without pay for stealing a *headlight?"*

Angeramo bent back over his report. "No, Gabe. For getting *caught* stealing a headlight."

Dunn was disappointed. Trinidad was getting sloppy. "You know, Carl, twenty-six doesn't really need headlights. They're always at dinner."

"Thank you, Gabe." Angeramo didn't look up.

"You ever work the twenty-six car? The indentation in the driver's seat is so deep you can barely see over the wheel."

This time Angeramo looked up. Dunn excused himself to make a phone call.

The police officer's credo is: *A good cop does not get cold, wet, or hungry.* By this measure, North Salem, the twenty-six car beat, had some of the best cops on the force.

Chairs scraped and the young lady sat down. Dunn folded his hands and looked at her. He had more circumstantial evidence than he knew what to do with. It was time to break the alibi. Hopefully by lunchtime.

"OK, Adele. When we first talked, you said Eugene was with you all of Friday night. Saturday morning, did you come down with him to the station to get Chris?"

Adele didn't look like she thought she could pull this off. "No."

"So he wasn't with you all Saturday morning then," Dunn said.

"It only took a few minutes."

"To bail somebody out? Afraid not. They have to locate the clerk on call, wait for him to come down, Chris would have to sign papers. More than a few minutes, Adele. Did Eugene have the money on him? Or did you have it laying around the house?"

She didn't respond. *Steadfast. I can be steadfast.*

"Adele, we know exactly what time Eugene showed up here. Do you? Can you tell me when he left? Even approximately?"

She shrugged. "Who keeps track of the time on Saturday morning? Could have been seven, eight, ten . . . I wouldn't have noticed. Or even cared."

"And we're supposed to believe that you noticed how long he was gone?" Dunn asked.

"Yes. It was just long enough to pick up Chris. It wasn't enough time to kill Moira," the girl said.

"Doesn't take much time to put a bullet through a head. Plenty of time for that."

"But not to type a note. Not the way Eugene types."

Dunn was quiet. After a moment he said softly: "How'd you know there was a typed note?"

Her eyes widened. "One of you must have mentioned it to Eugene, or to Chris?"

Good try. "No, we did not. Only to her family."

She pulled out a cigarette pack that looked like it had been sat on.

Dunn bent forward. "Hate to tell you, kid, but you're not going to do Eugene much good. You'll be perjuring yourself for nothing. Ever been to jail? Is he worth it?"

She fingered her necklace. Her machine cranked away for a few seconds. Then the grand total came up. What's in it for Adele? "OK, OK," she said, and made herself more comfortable in the chair. The recitative was over. Time for the aria.

Mallory was out of intensive care and surrounded by flowers and plants in a room he shared with a man who looked like he hadn't made it. Myles appeared in the doorway in a shirt that would wake the dead and with a bottle of something more cheering than African violets.

"Hey, handsome!" he shouted. The man in the next bed startled.

Mallory opened his eyes. "Hey, Jake. Buddy."

"How're you doing? North Salem's gotten worse than the Point since you left. Rampant crime. All the elderly, the women, the children, are crying for your return, lapper."

Mallory smiled. "I'm recovering, they tell me."

Myles pulled up a chair. "You'd damn well better. Lot of broken hearts if you left us. What would all those babies do for a father? Think of all the obstetricians in Salem who depend on you for dinner."

Mallory wondered if recovery was a good thing. "Did they get the guy who stuck me?"

Myles nodded and handed him the brown bag. "He didn't get far. Lynn picked him up. But we made it easy for them. We wore him down. Half the force was on his tail. He couldn't run too long with a smashed arm. The guy was on coke, all fucked up, angry as hell."

"*Half* the force? I saw every car pull up . . . everybody was there, Jake . . ."

"Oh, those guys?" Myles sniffed. "They weren't there for you. They were taking dinner breaks. Heard the food was good in North Salem."

Mallory looked hurt. "How's Gabe doing? Cleared his case yet?"

"As we speak, sir. As we speak. I think he's questioning some mystery witness. I saw him hunting around for the rubber hose earlier."

Mallory looked distracted. "So the guy's in jail? The one who got me?"

"Room at the inn, pal," Myles assured him. "Room at the inn."

"He got in around five, I guess. Five in the morning," Adele said, after a long drag on her cigarette. Dunn reached across to Myles's desk and grabbed a ceramic sombrero ashtray. He had given away his own ashtrays two years ago. But he still wasn't over the longing.

"Did he say where he had been?" Five was stretching it for the time of death. The girl flicked an ash into the brim of the hat. "On a job." *Guy's gotta work . . .*

"Then what?"

"I gave him the message that Chris was down here. He had something to eat, changed his clothes, then left. He said he'd have to find some cash."

"When did you next see him?" Dunn asked.

"Close to nine. He had dropped Chris off to get cleaned

up. Came back to my place, slept for about an hour, then
he called Chris and told him to meet him over at Moira's."

"Why?"

"I think he said something about moving some stuff.
Cards. He was worried the cops would come sniffing
around after Judd put them, put you, on Chris's trail. Eugene didn't think Moira's place was safe anymore. They
used to keep stuff down under her garage. No one goes
down there. I heard it's like a maze of little rooms and
pipes and stuff. They coulda hid a Porsche down there and
you guys would never have found it."

Well, sometimes our boys get a little sloppy, Dunn
thought.

Adele continued: "Then a little later, he left."

"How long was he gone?"

"A couple of hours. He came back with a box. Then he
told me Moira was dead. He said Chris went in to see her
after they got their stuff and found her on the living-room
floor. Then Eugene started saying things like, he shouldn't
have left him alone that hour after they left the station. He
asked me if Moira and Chris had fought recently. Trying to
make me suspect Chris, I guess."

"Did you?"

Adele shook her head. "Not Chris. No way. Eugene
even told me later that Moira had taken some of the cards.
Some of the really valuable ones. He thought Chris might
have noticed and so killed Moira. I told him I just couldn't
believe that."

"What was his reaction?" Dunn asked.

"I guess he gave up on that line. Later, he told me not to
mention anything to Chris about the missing cards. You
know what I think?"

Dunn put his hands behind his head and leaned back.

Adele continued: "I think he knew where Moira hid the
cards. And I think he wasn't going to tell Chris. Chris

didn't know anything about baseball cards anyway. He wouldn't have noticed."

Dishonor among thieves. Dunn actually was beginning to feel sorry for Chris. All that talent. But the guy could pick real lulus for partners.

"Why didn't they split up the cards when they got them?" Dunn asked her.

"I think they were out of time. Eugene said it took so long to peel the safe, and he had to be somewhere on the South Shore Friday morning. They divided up the cash. He said the cards would take a long time, there were so many of them. Chris trusted Eugene. So it was no big deal."

Dunn smiled. It was like watching a cashier close out her register. The tape just kept cranking out numbers. One transaction after another. Tallying up. Adele was describing it like she had been there taking notes. "Couldn't Chris have been the one to take the cards?" he asked.

"He wouldn't have been that stupid. Anyway, Chris is honorable." She spoke with reverence. Dunn was beginning to understand. "You know, he always splits the take evenly, with his driver or lookout. And he does all the work. He used to tell me, they share the risk, they share the reward." Her eyes were shining. "And he doesn't do houses anymore. Not since he was a kid. Chris doesn't like hurting individual people."

The owner of the Sports King had no insurance. He had been an individual. He was hurting. But Dunn was familiar with this rationale. A lot of establishments exaggerate their insurance claims, often getting back considerably more than they lose.

"A great guy," Dunn said. He had nearly wrapped up his murder. The B&E's were falling into place. Now he felt exhausted. With all the overtime the past five days, he was looking forward to a few days off. Couple of people he wanted to see. One required clear weather, one didn't.

Also needed to dig up a lawyer. One more interview to go first. And a warrant.

She looked up at him. "What's going to happen to him?"

Dunn knew she was thinking of Chris, not Eugene. He shrugged. "It depends. He's looking at some time, for certain. But how much time—that's partly up to him. I like getting merchandise back. Baseball cards—that would make me very happy. Maybe he'll just go in long enough to get his teeth fixed and pick up his new shoes." He looked down at his three-year-old Reeboks, now once again dry. "They always get better shoes than we do. I can tell you one thing," he added. "He'll be out long before Eugene."

An important quality in a man.

On his way to get the warrant, Dunn thought about Mel. Much like thinking about summer vacation just before your last final exam. He had known this woman for nearly a year. Was he bringing to the development of close relationships the same skill and speed he brought to flying lessons? Which in turn rivaled his development of reading skills. Nothing is easy. Damn boulder keeps slipping.

Chapter 35

Squeeze Play

"Why'd you kill her?" Dunn asked Sollors late Wednesday in the inner sanctum after the usual formalities.

Thunder assaulted the night like cannons from the "1812 Overture." A fast-moving cold front embedded with a band of thunder showers was sweeping the North Shore and clearing the previous night's snow from the runways at Beverly Airport. The music of the storm was appropriate, thought Dunn, as the Great Detective Procures the Confession in the Parlor. Only the rest of the suspects were not assembled; his only audience was Keith Gagnon of the State Police CPAC unit, who had failed in his attempt to take control, but was doing all right taking notes. Sometimes the state could be a big help.

And Angeramo's office was no parlor, though the miniature dart board on the opposite wall lent a cozy note of competency to the department. A slotted cookie tin decorated with poinsettias on the corner of the desk labeled "OVERTIME" attested to their superior organization.

Eugene Sollors sat across from him, smooth, tanned, and Mirandized. With Adele's help, a search warrant had been obtained for Sollors's apartment. The box of cards was not found, although the Satchel Paige was recovered. With Chris Alexei's half, and the seven Moira had taken, Mr. Lazarus was considering himself pretty lucky. Sollors refused to disclose the whereabouts of the rest; his long-term disability benefits, he called it.

Also found in the apartment were an orphan work glove, some checks endorsed to the Witch's Brew, and bits of charred paper clinging to the inside of the trash can. By the few discernible typed letters, they appeared to be from the first draft of the note found at Moira's.

"She stole my cards," stated Sollors, with his ever sunny smile.

"Your cards?" Dunn felt disappointment creeping in. Was that all this was going to be about? A 1953 Bowman Willie Mays? A Mickey Mantle rookie card?

"We did the work, not her."

"She told you how to get them back, right? She even must have described the envelope for you."

"The red one. Yeah. Only one she had that they'd fit in." He stretched out his legs.

"So why shoot her?" the detective asked again.

"I didn't mean to kill her, actually. She had the gun out when I first got into the house. She heard me coming in and got scared. So first I had to get it away from her. Then I had to get her to talk. But after that, when I lowered the gun, she wasn't scared anymore. Then she was sorry she told me and got mad. She said if I took the cards away from her sister, she'd turn me in. Moira had all kinds of stuff on me. And she didn't mind bringing Chris down along with me. Two-faced bitch. No way was I gonna let her send me to jail. We argued, I got ripped, really mad at her, and . . . scared. I got scared."

The girl had no sense. Yelling at some motherfucker who's holding a gun to your head? Maybe she was trying to commit suicide after all. But then why disclose the whereabouts of the cards? Perhaps one's first instinct is survival after all. And stupidity is a close second.

"Jail's that bad? To kill her over?" asked the detective.

"The Glee Club was OK. Everything else sucked," Sollors said. "But the main thing . . . the main thing is, I'd lose Adele."

Oops, thought Dunn. Man kills woman to keep another he's already lost. And to recover booty that was never his. He cocked his head. "What was the other shot for, Eugene?"

Sollors looked down at his hands. "The first one didn't leave any traces on her hands. Powder burns. I mean, it wasn't planned. An accident, really. So even though it was risky I thought I should fire a second shot, with her hand around mine."

"It was a nice touch," said Dunn. *We struggled and the gun went off. Then I panicked and planned the perfect coverup.* Dunn didn't mention that the mixed ammo had been the boy's undoing. It would come out in court. "When did you discover the cards were missing?" he asked.

"Chris called Adele from jail Friday night. He told her to get ahold of me—I could get cash to bail him out. I found out early the next morning. But I decided it would be a good idea first to move the cards as soon as I could. I didn't know what Chris might be telling you guys.

"So I went to Moira's and come to find out someone had been messing with them. I just got a little suspicious, you know, so I checked on a few of the high-priced ones. They're usually in plastic protectors that screw together. Well, the protectors were there, still with the original price tags. But I spotted immediately that the cards were the wrong ones. Someone had taken seven or eight of my best cards and replaced them with some of the cheap ones. Well, it wasn't Chris. He had an alibi. And he had principles. But *Moira.* Little Miss Hypocrite. Too good for us, you know? Couldn't accept tainted gifts anymore. Throwing Chris over, looking for an honest man. Honest, like her."

The only thing worse than a thief was a dirty double-crossing thief. Dunn asked: "But she must have known you'd miss them?"

"Sooner or later, yeah. I think she thought she was buying time by switching the protectors. She didn't have any idea how much I know cards. I wasn't fooled for a second. After our . . . argument, after Moira was dead, I put the box of cards back. Less chance Chris would suspect me if we came for the cards together. And then found her together."

Dunn nodded. "So, what was she buying time for, Eugene?"

Sollors leaned back. "I think she had a plan. I think she was going to dime us out. Turn us in. Cops recover the box of cards. Some's missing, they assume we already sold them. Who's gonna believe us? Chris and me are behind bars. Old man gets most of his cards back. And Moira and her sister are suddenly out of debt. And Moira goes back to being an honest woman."

An honest woman. Trying to grow a new life like she grew new carrots. But instead gets a jar of murky water. Pain with no relief. Hope chest with no hope. Wings with no feathers. And she crashes on takeoff.

Dunn wondered what Sasha would have done if Moira's plan had worked. Paid off her car? Or done her civic duty. For a very large number of folks, the essential thing that keeps them honest is lack of opportunity.

In the end, she might have come forward. And Moira might have changed her mind by light of day. Dunn thought it would be nice to believe that.

Chapter 36

Epilogue

"Done a lot of details this week?" Zack suddenly yelled out over the engine. Dunn jumped and the plane dipped.

"No. Somebody died."

The instructor bellowed with laughter. "Gabe, get a life!"

The policeman shuddered. *Good Life—Good Death.*

On final for Dunn's third touch and go, Zack suggested radioing the tower and requesting a full stop landing instead. Dunn landed and pulled off onto the taxiway. As he slowed to switch radio frequencies, Zack suddenly yanked open the door and heaved his bulk out onto the tarmac. "Why don't you take it around a couple times?" He walked a safe distance onto the grass and lit up a cigarette.

Dunn yelled out to him. "I suppose you want to be paid for this break, you sonofabitch."

Zack smiled. Dunn taxied the Cessna back to the active runway and radioed the tower.

In a moment he was airborne. Alone.